TALKING TO

GREEN TREE LEAVES

MEMOIR OF

Kenneth Leon Little, Sr.

Second Edition

ISBN 978-1-7345808-6-0 (Paperback)

ISBN 978-1-7345808-9-1 (eBook)

Printed in the United States of America

ACKNOWLEDGMENTS

A huge thank you goes out to Angel Little, my wife, my lover, my best friend and my confidant. Angel spent numerous hours editing and critiquing my book. Through my tears and frustration, Angel made sure I stayed the course in writing about good and bad experiences in my life. She constantly reminded me that my documented experiences could be a guiding light for someone to follow to break out family cycles of mental, physical and verbal abuse and societal racism. I thank her for her unyielding encouragement and support.

Barbara Smith-Reed, my licensed counselor and long-time friend for over 25 years. I salute her untiring dedication to support me and numerous other Vietnam Veterans. I thank her for being a keeper of secrets and guiding me through numerous dark life events. I tremble when I think about how I wasted years reflecting on my troubled life by staring at the rear-view mirror. Thanks to her exceptional professional counseling, I now celebrate life by looking forward for blessings through life's huge windshield. Her edit and critique of my book were fantastic.

Fola Kayode, was my licensed counselor for over three years. Early on, I talked to her about my life's peaks and valleys. When we discussed my negative life experiences, she encouraged me to focus on positive outcomes. I soon realized that the positive aspects of my life far outweighed the negative. She then nick-named me, "Resilient," and underscored how I recovered from numerous misfortunes. I thank her for her counsel and support.

CHAPTER 1

INTRODUCTION

I hope and pray that my memoir encourages people of all backgrounds and ages who are subjected to a cycle of physical, verbal, and domestic abuse and racism to stay the course in pursuing their dreams and visions. Breaking these horrible cycles starts with you. Please do not let fear become your enemy.

Growing up, I had a very dysfunctional family. There was evidence of untreated mental health issues, adultery, and spousal and child abuse. Although I endured countless years of abuse, from childhood to adulthood, I nurtured fascinating dreams and visions for a better life. My dreams and visions resonated in my mind and heart both day and night.

My initial dreams and visions included venturing out of my present environment to look for love, travel the world, join the military, get a college degree, get a great-paying white-collar job, get married, buy a house, and have a loving family. With God's help, I did not allow segregation in the 1960s and future years to stop me from moving forward toward my dreams and visions. I dealt with overt (open) or covert (hidden) racism. A loving person once said to me, "If you cannot see past your circumstances, then your circumstances become your destiny."

CHILDHOOD AND DOMESTIC ABUSE

As a child, I often wondered, how was it possible for me to love my mother and strongly dislike her character? Strangely enough, she did not allow anyone other than herself to abuse me.

In my developmental years, there was a vicious cycle of domestic abuse in my family. My mother suffered from a severe untreated mental health condition and was born under the astrological sign of Gemini. I was deeply concerned about my mother's well-being as she displayed narcissistic behavior. In other words, she believed that she was the only important person in the world. My mother often took her mental frustrations out on me. She would physically beat me with objects such as tree branches, leather belts, wet dishcloths, and others. As a result, she beat the self-esteem out of me.

HOW TELEVISION (TV) INFLUENCED MY DREAMS AND VISIONS

Growing up in the 1960s, I loved watching selected shows on my family's small-screen black-and-white TV. A large TV antenna was placed on top of the house and attached to the chimney. Sometimes, to gain better TV reception, especially during cloudy weather, my father would hoist me up so I could climb on top of the house and slowly rotate the antenna.

We only had access to three different TV channels in the rural area. I loved turning off the ceiling light in the living room, sitting on the floor and pretending to be in a movie theater.

Two TV shows really had tremendous impact on my dreams and visions. First, I loved watching Leave It to Beaver. Although the characters were acting, I admired their family structure (father, mother, and two children). When family members interacted with one another in a civil manner, it made me fantasize. I dreamed of having a similar family structure (father, mother, and two children) that encourages them to interact with one another in a civil manner. Secondly, I loved watching The Adventures of Ozzie and Harriet. I also admired their family structure. My focus on the show was watching and listening to their son, Ricky Nelson, singing beautiful songs and playing his guitar. One song he recorded and sang was "Traveling Man." When he sang the lyrics "I'm a traveling man, I mentally made a lot of stops all over the world," these words ignited my dreams and visions of traveling around the world.

During that era, there were limited TV shows with black actors. One exception was Amos 'n' Andy. These actors performed slapstick comedy and cast black people's image in an unintelligent, negative light.

TRAUMATIC PSYCHOLOGICAL EVENTS WITH MY MOTHER

I encountered numerous traumatic experiences with my mother. Two major events still stand out in my mind. The first event was, when I was five years old, my mother had a psychotic break down. During a bright, sunshiny day, we started walking down a dark old backwoods country road in Mount Gilead, North Carolina. There were tall pine trees on both sides of the road. The pine tree needles were wavering in the wind. While tightly holding my hand, my mother started cursing and accusing me of causing her to have a nervous breakdown. I was so afraid and cried out of control. I really wanted to undo whatever I had done as a child to cause her nervous breakdown.

The second event, I received a devastating letter from my

mother while I was in the US Army and stationed in Vietnam. She wrote, "I hope you get killed in Vietnam so I can collect the $10,000 military insurance policy. You caused me to have a nervous breakdown, and you do not deserve to live!" I was traumatized after reading her letter. For a short time, her letter made me question my self-worth. Fortunately, mentally I marched on and continued to be a soldier in Vietnam.

MY PHYSICAL AND MENTAL HEALTH

During my childhood, I was extremely underweight and experienced numerous physical and mental health problems. My physical health problems included rheumatic fever, a ruptured appendix, a very nervous stomach, and constant headaches. My mental health problems included low self-esteem, low self-worth, poor social skills, and constantly living under a dark cloud of domestic abuse.

MY MOTHER'S EXTRAMARITAL AFFAIRS AND PHYSICAL ABUSE

My mother was relentless in getting involved in numerous extra-marital affairs. The result: my father was constantly physically abusing her. There was also mama, daddy, and baby drama. Was the man who raised me my real father? My father appeared to be very distant with me. He was very stern and had a no-nonsense personality. It was nerve-racking for me to helplessly watch my parents' mean behavior toward each other and me. At a very young age, I dreamed of the day when I could stop riding this nerve-racking merry-go-round.

CHAPTER 2

MY TALL SYCAMORE TREE

MY TEMPORARY ESCAPE FROM MENTAL, PHYSICAL, AND DOMESTIC ABUSE

To temporarily escape mental and physical abuse and domestic violence in the house, I would go outside and climb a tall American sycamore tree. The tall tree had a grayish bark and massive green leaves that were up to seven inches long and broad. The average height of the sycamore ranged from eighty to one hundred feet. I climbed high into the tall tree, positioned my body on the tree's strongest boughs, and slightly locked my legs around the center portion of the tree. This was a comforting and meditating position.

The tall tree was in the backyard of our house that was located in a rural area of New London, North Carolina. The reason the tree grew so tall, with massive green leaves, was that its lengthy tree roots gravitated and absorbed fertilizer from the family's private septic tank or sewage line. In most rural areas, it was common for houses to have private septic tanks.

While I was in the tall tree, the massive green tree leaves

served as my fortress and provided an escape from reality. I felt safe. The green leaves became my alter ego or trusted companions. It was therapeutic for me to talk to the green tree leaves about my frustrations. I had a trusting relationship with them. It had to be God speaking to me through the massive green tree leaves.

On some days, the blowing wind rocked the tall tree back and forth. This had a very soothing and cradling effect on me. I imagined the green leaves tightly wrapping me in their midst and comforting my mind, soul, and spirit. I inhaled fresh air from the blowing wind and exhaled my inner frustrations. Sometimes, while relaxing in the tall tree, I closed my eyes and envisioned my spirit floating away from my body and walking among the soft, fluffy white clouds. I really wanted my physical body to connect with my spirit and walk among the peaceful clouds. After my therapy sessions with the green tree leaves, I often had positive thoughts of a better life. They advised me to be patient and have faith in God, as hard times would eventually mold me into a strong, resilient, and responsible man.

GOD CARRIED ME

As I grew older, I realized that through adversities or my down-in-the-valley experiences in life, God was molding and shaping me to become a strong, resilient, and responsible man. Each time I overcame adversity, life got sweeter. Although I strayed off course at times, God guided me back on course in pursing my dreams and visions.

God blessed me to have loving grandparents in my life, Grandfather and Grandmother Little and Grandfather and Grandmother Gould. They gave me love and a firm foundation to face life's challenges. In short, they served as stable bridges over troubled waters flowing in and out of my life. I still love and miss them dearly.

To date, I still feel their love flowing down on me from heaven. For example, when I walk in the rain, I feel it cleansing my mind, soul, body, and spirit. The cleansing raindrops wash away my fears and life's challenges, and when I walk in the sun, it feels like the radiant cosmic (spiritual) sunbeams warm my spirit, inspire bright and new growth, and serve as my life's guiding light. I love and miss my grandparents dearly!

CHAPTER 3

MY LIFE EVOLVED FROM FORTHCOMING LIFE LESSONS

OVERVIEW OF MOUNT GILEAD, NORTH CAROLINA: MY BIRTHPLACE

I was born in the late 1940s in this small Southern agricultural town named Mount Gilead, North Carolina, located just off Highway 109. I was born in an old grayish-colored, weather-beaten wooden house. We had an outdoor toilet and retrieved water from a hand-operated pump located in the backyard, near the vegetable garden. This water was used for drinking, bathing, washing clothes and dishes, and cleaning the house. It was also drinking water for pigs my father raised for food.

During the summer months, it was extremely hot inside the house. The black cast-iron wood-stove generated a lot of heat when my parents cooked daily meals. During the winter months, the frigid wind swirled freely throughout the whole house. The wood-burning fireplace was supposed to heat the house; however, most of the heat evaporated up through the old redbrick chimney. It was so cold in my bedroom at night I had to get fully dressed to go to bed. My parents put layers of heavy homemade quilts on the bed to keep me warm. I could see my breath each time I exhaled in the cold bedroom.

There was an uneven red dirt driveway leading to the old house. My father's car got stuck in red mud during heavy rains. However, in rainy summer months, it was soothing to hear rain dancing on the house's tin roof. Whether it was day or night, the sound of rain falling on the tin roof lulled me to sleep. When rolling thunder and flashing lightning accompanied heavy rain, I crawled under the bed for security.

THE TOWNSPEOPLE

Most of the townspeople were extremely poor. To escape the poverty-stricken town, when most of the town's young people became of age, they migrated from Mount Gilead to northeast cities, such as Washington, DC; Baltimore, Maryland; Philadelphia, Pennsylvania; and New York, New York in search of a better life.

Back then, most of the people who remained in Mount Gilead worked as sharecroppers with the descendants of former plantation slave owners, while others worked inside their big "white" houses. Descendants of former plantation slave owners inherited the big "white" houses. A select few of the black people were independent farmers who grew marketable items to sell, such as cotton, corn, tobacco, cucumbers, cantaloupes, watermelons, and others. According to Grandfather Little, black farmers were paid less money than white farmers.

During that time, there were limited good-paying jobs in cotton mills and manufacturing plants for black people. To survive, they worked in cotton and tobacco fields and peach orchards from sunup to sundown. People who lived on former plantation slave owners' property lived rent-free in run-down, substandard old housing. For example, one could sit in the living room, look down through cracks in the floor, and see chickens walking around underneath the house.

My family was fortunate in that my father had a good-paying job working for Alcoa Aluminum Company in Badin, North Carolina. He drove an old green manual-shift Chevrolet from Mount Gilead to Badin each workday. His travel time was around thirty minutes each way. My mother was a stay-at-home housewife.

MOUNT GILEAD'S ECONOMY: BOOTLEGGERS AND MOONSHINERS

We had a white neighbor named Mr. Joe who owned a bootlegger's house located directly across our old house on Highway 109. The bootlegger's house was divided into two parts for patrons: "white only" and "colored only." On weekends, he sold illegal moonshine liquor, beer, fried chicken sandwiches, and pickled pig's feet. On several occasions, my parents took me into the "colored only" side of the bootlegger's house. They drank illegal moonshine liquor and beer and ate fried chicken sandwiches and pickled pig's feet. They laughed and danced to loud jukebox music. I sat on the floor in a dark corner of the room and quietly laughed at intoxicated black people trying to dance to loud music.

Chicken bones, pickled pig's feet bones, greasy wax paper, and empty beer cans littered the dirty floor. If loud arguments or fights erupted among customers, Mr. Joe retrieved his twelve-gauge shotgun to restore order.

Bootleggers and moonshiners played an important role in Mount Gilead's economy. The wealthiest people in Mount

Gilead were plantation owners, bootleggers, and moonshiners. Moonshiners made and sold illegal moonshine (white corn liquor) to bootleggers. In turn, bootleggers sold the moonshine liquor to customers. Moonshiners and bootleggers did not pay taxes on large profits generated from illegal liquor sales.

Moonshiners made illegal moonshine during summer months in isolated, wooded areas near flowing streams of water. They built and set up liquor stills (large copper kettle for processing liquor) under trees with thick leaves to camouflage their night activities. Water was used to cool large cooper pots while cooking liquor. The moon provided light for moonshiners at night. Thus, the term moonshine liquor evolved.

Going to jail or prison was a revolving door for moonshiners and bootleggers. They were apprehended by police officers, served time in jail or prison, got out, and made and sold illegal moonshine again.

A few of my wealthy family members mastered the craft of making and selling illegal moonshine. These relatives were from my Gould family bloodline, such as my uncles, aunts, and cousins. It was a family business. They owned nice cars, houses, and large farms with livestock.

I remember visiting and spending weekends in their homes. Each room in the house had beautiful, well-crafted furniture. They were very nice and always cooked delicious food. I was banned from the special, spacious room in the house as this was where they sold alcohol to their customers. They also had a jukebox in the room for customers to listen to music and dance.

Rumor has it that moonshiners and bootleggers' valuables and properties were listed in their wives' names to prevent the government from confiscating them.

According to townspeople, years ago, bootleggers, moonshiners, and church ministers conspired to prevent formal businesses from selling legal liquor by the drink in Mount Gilead. They further stated that church ministers were paid to lobby politicians to vote against selling legal liquor by the drink. This kept illegal moonshine liquor flowing.

CHAPTER 4

MOTHER-FATHER-SON DRAMA

MY MOTHER'S MENTAL HEALTH DRAMA

I was a skinny brown-skinned boy, and I often wondered why my muscular tall light-skinned father never really embraced me as his son. He smiled a lot and had a very quiet demeanor. Quite often, he was stern and never showed any real affection toward me. Maybe he was confused since I strongly resembled my mother and her Gould family relatives. Or maybe he was just frustrated with his relationship with my mother.

When I was five, one hot summer day, my mother put on her favorite light-blue coat, grabbed my hand, and started walking down a shady country road in Mount Gilead, North Carolina. She mumbled to herself and finally looked at me and screamed, "Ken, it's your fault that I had a damn nervous breakdown!" I cried as I was confused about my mother's anger. Just then, Mr. Jones, a local neighbor, was driving by, stopped, and forced me and my mother into his car. She continued shouting and blaming me for her mental condition.

My father was at work at Alcoa in Badin, North Carolina, so Mr. Jones drove us to my paternal grandparents' house in Mount Gilead, North Carolina. My mother then shouted and blamed Grandfather and Grandmother Little for her mental condition. This became a long-lasting strained relationship. A lengthy period went by before my mother allowed me to spend nights at my estranged grandparents' house.

My mother continually blamed me for her mental health condition, and I concluded that she did not love me. Back in the 1950s, most people who suffered from mental health conditions were left untreated. Most were in denial regarding their mental health condition and wanted to avoid being labeled crazy by the community.

When my mother drank alcohol, her mental illness magnified. It was like throwing a lighted match on gasoline. In public, my mother talked aloud, bragging about her physical beauty, clothes, and shoes. Without reason, she cursed at people and attacked their character and openly flirted with men in front of their wives.

From a layman's perspective, and based on research extracted from Google, by today's mental health standards, my mother would have been diagnosed as having a bipolar disorder. Research notes that bipolar disorder is defined as a mental illness classified as a mood disorder. Research further states that people who suffer from episodes of extreme agitation tend to suffer from episodes of depression, also known as manic-depressive disorder. Research underscores that an episode of mania is usually identified by a set of behavioral changes. These changes include impulsive behavior, such as excessive spending, hyper-sexuality, and other symptoms.

CHAPTER 5

MY MOTHER'S CHILDHOOD

GOULD FAMILY HISTORY

I learned from my mother that Grandfather Gould's parents were slaves of white plantation owners with the surname Gould. After the United States (US) government supposedly freed slaves in 1865, my great grandparents continued to use the former plantation owners' surname.

On a few of my mother's happy days, she talked to me about her childhood years growing up on a farm in Mount Gilead. She asserted, "I hated the hardship I experienced being the daughter of a sharecropper farmer. I worked in cotton fields and cornfields from sunup to sundown. My father gave me brutal beatings if I had a slow day performing manual labor in the field."

She further asserted, to add insult to injury, "If Mr. Gould, the white plantation owner, saw me getting on the school bus, he cursed at my father for allowing me to go to school. He also threatened to reduce my father's already low sharecropper income." She then said that when the plantation owner was not watching, she sneaked onto the school bus and went to school.

My mother often bragged about winning a spelling bee in the sixth grade, and she told me neighbors celebrated when she won the spelling bee. She said, "They picked me up and carried me off the stage!" She also said, "I went on to become a high school basketball star. My team won several state basketball championships."

She told me that during her tenth-grade year, she dropped out of high school to marry my father.

I recall seeing pictures of my mother when she was young. She was extremely beautiful. She had a smooth brown complexion and stood five feet seven inches tall, with long black hair. On many occasions, she bragged that her body resembled the shape of a Coca-Cola bottle. When in public, she wore expensive, stylish clothes and commanded attention when she walked into a room.

My mother was extremely confident, smart, and full of wisdom and had a keen spirit of discernment. She had a gift of immediately reading a person's body language and personality. She did not take any "wooden nickels". Her greatest passion was feeding hungry children when they were in her presence. This passion grew out of her childhood experience of going hungry on selected Sundays at the Gould family house.

GRANDFATHER GOULD'S FAMILY ABUSE

In yet another rare civil conversation, my mother told me more about her turbulent childhood. She labeled Grandfather Gould as a gangster preacher. He got into fights and always carried a .38-caliber pistol in his pocket. He also had knife cut scars on his body.

Based on my mother's information, she said one day, at lunch-time, she and Grandfather Gould left the cotton field and walked home to eat. When they walked into the house, they caught Grandmother Gould and a neighbor named Mr. Jody having sex on the kitchen floor. Grandfather Gould quickly retrieved his twelve-gauge shotgun and said, "I am going to kill Mr. Jody."

Grandmother Gould's defense was "Mr. Jody used witchcraft to control and make me have sex with him."

My mother said, "Although I was fearful of your grandfather, I grabbed the shotgun, screamed, and begged him not to kill Mr. Jody." My mother's action gave Mr. Jody a chance to run out of the house and escape death. Grandfather Gould viewed my mother's actions as being disrespectful. As punishment that night, he made my mother sleep in bed with the loaded shotgun under her pillow. From that day forward, she claimed to be fearful of firearms.

My mother shared another strange situation she experienced with Grandfather Gould. She said one day, Grandfather Gould was riding on a dark-brown-colored mule home from the cotton field because of bad weather. There was a heavy downpour of rain, loud-rumbling thunder, and flashes of lightning lit up the dark sky. As he rode the mule toward the house, a bolt of lightning struck and killed the mule instantly. Grandfather Gould was unharmed; God spared his life that day. She stated that after what should have been a remarkable, life-changing experience for my grandfather, he continued to be a very mean person.

Remembering these experiences my mother shared with me concerning Grandfather Gould triggered an aha moment for me. That is, my mother learned or inherited child abuse from my grandfather—it was a vicious cycle.

MY MOTHER'S BEST TEENAGE GIRLFRIEND

My mother also explained her strained relationship with her older brother, Jacob. He dated her best teenage girlfriend and basketball teammate named Louise. Uncle Jacob got her pregnant, but she suddenly died from pregnancy complications.

After her death, my mother was extremely livid and harbored deep resentment toward Uncle Jacob. He became a nonentity in her life. I always viewed Uncle Jacob as a quiet, hardworking gentleman. It was hard for me to believe they grew up in the same house.

SUNDAY DINNERS AT THE GOULD FAMILY HOUSE

My mother told me that she resented her father's gangster-preacher buddies. They would come to her house after church for dinner, and eat all the fried chicken, potato salad, green beans, corn bread, and dessert my grandmother cooked for dinner.

My mother said, after dinner, she would hide in the tobacco barn and watch Grandfather Gould and his preacher buddies drink illegal moonshine white liquor from mason jars. She overheard them talking about light-skinned black women (affectionately called red-bones) who had keen facial features and long black hair. She said they lusted after and dated single and married women in churches and others who lived in various surrounding communities. These women possessed physical features they inherited from their white biological fathers (former plantation slave owners).

My mother was angry as she, her brother, and her mother did not have food to eat. She was also angry because Grandmother Gould was very passive regarding the food situation and did not challenge my grandfather or the visiting preachers for eating all the food. My mother became very emotional when she said Grandfather Gould had a long history of physically and verbally abusing his family.

MY MOTHER AND FATHER ELOPED: NEWLYWEDS' ISSUES

My mother said she was sixteen and my father was twenty-two years old when they eloped and got married. She said when she returned home the next day, she got an unmerciful beating from Grandfather Gould for eloping. Grandmother Gould kicked her out of the Gould family house. My mother was forced to live with her new in-laws, the Little family.

According to my mother, Grandfather and Grandmother Little viewed her as a gold digger who wanted to get away from her dysfunctional Gould family. My mother said that this quickly became a very sensitive situation as the Little family did not think she was worthy of their hardworking son.

My father had an extremely light-skinned complexion, was tall and handsome, and had a strong muscular build. He often had a smile on his face. Because of his muscular build, his friends nick-named him Big Doc. Although my father dropped out of school in the eighth grade, he had a good-paying blue-collar job working for Alcoa Aluminum Company in Badin, North Carolina.

GRANDMOTHER GOULD LEAVES GRANDFATHER GOULD TO ESCAPE ABUSE

In the early 1940s, the United States entered World War II with its allies to fight in Germany, Italy, Japan, and others. It was family gossip that around this time, Grandmother Gould moved from Mount Gilead, North Carolina, to Newport News, Virginia.

Family members said Grandfather Gould had physically and verbally abused Grandmother Gould for the last time in Mount Gilead. She packed her suitcases and moved to Newport News with her sister and brother-in-law.

Word has it Grandfather Gould left his sharecropper farm in Mount Gilead and moved to Newport News to beg Grandmother Gould not to end the marriage. They soon reunited.

GRANDFATHER AND GRANDMOTHER GOULD'S NEW JOBS

After the United States entered World War II, it had to become battle ready to fight the enemy by building large aircraft carriers, battleships, and submarines. Because of Grandfather Gould's muscular build, he was hired instantly to work at Newport News Shipbuilders (Shipyard) as a chipper. Chippers use highly compressed air hoses, jackhammers, and sharp iron wedges to remove excess hard metal from ships' bulkheads (walls) and decks (floors).

When chippers worked with jackhammers, they made loud noise while removing metal. The loud noise could damage chippers' eardrums and affect their hearing ability. They chipped metal for eight to ten hours on their knees each workday in cold and hot weather. It was backbreaking work yet muscle-building for chippers. Only black males worked as chippers, and white males were supervisors. However, the shipyard paid chippers high salaries to retain them.

Grandfather Gould's salary was excellent for a man who could not read or write. Make no mistake; he had a talent for adding and subtracting numbers and tracking and counting money. Grandmother Gould said she taught him how to sign his name on paychecks and other official documents. She also read Bible passages to him. He, in turn, memorized Bible passages to preach church sermons.

In the early days, my grandparents lived in a segregated (colored-only) neighborhood in Newport News called Newsome Park. They lived in a white duplex house owned by the shipyard.

Grandmother Gould worked as a maid for a rich white family in the Newport News suburbs. She hated the low-paying, backbreaking job that forced her to get down on her hands and knees to scrub floors in the massive house. She always said to me, "Go to college and get a decent job." She encouraged me to seek a white-collar job.

GRANDFATHER GOULD'S NEW PREACHER BUDDIES

Grandfather Gould soon became friends with local preachers he met in the Newport News Shipyard. It was like déjà vu, them eating fried chicken, drinking good liquor, and dating light-skinned black women. These women possessed the same keen facial features as white women. It appeared that redbones were the women of choice during that era.

GRANDMOTHER GOULD REFLECTS ON HER LIFE

One day, Grandmother Gould was angry and talked to me about Grandfather Gould's extramarital affairs. She said that he came home late one night with red lipstick smeared on his white shirt. He claimed the red smear came from red peppermint candy he dropped on his shirt.

Grandmother Gould chuckled about her life with

Grandfather Gould and reflected on her teenage years growing up on a farm in Mount Gilead, North Carolina. She said, "I was a very pretty, short, and petite young brown-skinned lady with long black hair." She dropped out of elementary school after she learned to read and write.

She commented, "One Sunday afternoon, I was sitting on the front porch of my family's country house. That was when I noticed a handsome muscular brown-skinned, well-dressed man walking down the country road with a Bible in his hand. Your grandfather presented himself to me as a country preacher who did not curse, smoke, or drink alcohol." She admitted that she fell in love with his handsome looks and preacher image.

After a brief pause, she said, "Marrying your grandfather was the biggest mistake of my life." To avoid being judgmental, I just looked and gave her my "I love you" smile. The life lesson for me was an old cliché: "You cannot judge a book by its cover." Some people do project false images.

ADULT RELATIONSHIP ADVICE TO ME AS A TEENAGER

During my younger years, adults advised me to date and eventually marry a young lady who had high moral values and one who attended church regularly. Based on my experiences, the life lesson for me was, just because a person attends church regularly does not guarantee this person possesses high moral values. Again, I refer back to the old cliché "You cannot judge a book by its cover."

Life has taught me to establish a personal relationship with God through prayer and worship. My divine faith is being committed to God and not to earthy human beings. I now look to Him for spiritual guidance, favor, and wisdom. A minister once told a church congregation, "I do not know any earthy human being I have met in church who would submit to being crucified on a cross to demonstrate their love for me." Further, he stated, "Human beings do not have a heaven or hell to cast me in. Amen!"

CHAPTER 6

MY FATHER IS DRAFTED INTO THE US ARMY

As World War II was escalating, my father was drafted into the US Army. He had to leave his blue-collar job with Alcoa Aluminum Company in Badin, North Carolina. He was stationed in New York City after completing basic training and advanced infantry training. My mother said, "I was happy to move away from the Little family in Mount Gilead, North Carolina." She moved to New York City to join my father. Shortly thereafter, my father received military orders and was shipped to Germany to fight in the war.

My mother was eighteen years old when my father was fighting in Germany. My mother said, "I had to learn to survive alone for three years in New York City." The small monthly military allotment she received from my father was not sufficient to support her newfound New York lifestyle. She got two jobs, one working in a sewing factory during the day and another working at night as a cigarette girl in a prominent Harlem nightclub. She said she dressed and imitated classy New Yorkers.

My father served in the US Army as a combat infantry soldier during World War II. After the United States and its allies defeated Germany, Japan, and Italy, my father was honorably discharged from the army. He was a decorated soldier and awarded two Purple Heart medals for combat gunshot wounds.

According to my father, he sustained one gunshot wound at night after a black soldier in his unit gave their position away by lighting a cigarette. German soldiers fired their weapons and killed that soldier instantly and wounded my father. My father also said, "I was on patrol in the woods when I sustained the other gunshot wound. We engaged in a fierce firefight with German soldiers.

SOLDIERS' PSYCHOLOGICAL PROBLEMS

My father was proud of his military service in an all-black, segregated infantry unit. On rare occasions, he shared some of his military experiences with me. Sometimes at night, my father screamed out loud while having bad dreams about fighting in the war. After World War II, psychologists labeled soldiers with war-related psychological problems as being shell-shocked.

From a layman's point of view, psychologists today now recognize soldiers with the same psychological problems as suffering from post-traumatic stress disorder (PTSD). This condition is directly related to soldiers' horrific wartime experiences and can be treated by mental health professionals. Although my father's PTSD condition was never treated, I still wanted to be a soldier in the US Army like him.

MILITARY-STYLE DISCIPLINE

My father believed that every young man in the United States had an obligation to serve his country in the military. From my childhood, he groomed me to become a future soldier. I had to be respectful of adults and people of authority and was forbidden to stand around with my hands in my pockets. One rule my father strictly enforced was, when he assigned me a chore, I had to move out right then. One foot always had to be in motion.

For example, one afternoon my father told me to wash the dinner dishes. I responded, "That's a job for a girl!" He didn't say a word; he walked across the kitchen, grabbed me by my collar, and pushed my head up to the kitchen ceiling and stared at me. My tone and demeanor changed instantly during the few minutes I was dangling in the air. I begged him, "Please let me down, and I will wash the dishes and mop the floor!"

My father's action may be considered harsh by today's disciplinary standards for youth, but I never argued with him again. When he let me down, both my feet were in motion, running toward the kitchen sink to wash dishes!

These life lessons became a natural part of my being. Looking back, I realize now it was a blessing to have a strong disciplinarian as a father. From a personal perspective, I can tell receiving proper discipline in youth breeds resilient, responsible men and women.

CHAPTER 7

PARENTS DISAGREE ON RELOCATING FROM NEW YORK TO MOUNT GILEAD, NORTH CAROLINA

One day, I overheard my parents arguing about New York City. When my father returned home from the war, he paid my mother a surprise visit. He was surprised to find a man named Kenneth in the apartment—he ran out after seeing my father. My father was very angry and physically abused my mother.

After the dust settled, my parents then decided to make New York City their home. Because of overt (open) racism, my father could only find janitorial work in the city. During that era, black soldiers who served in World War II were not afforded the same recognition and opportunities as white soldiers. It is still a mystery to me why they were called the greatest generation. The most racist generation seems more appropriate.

After a few years went by, my father was really frustrated about their quality of life in New York City. However, my mother really enjoyed the glitz and glamour of New York City. Against my mother's wishes, they relocated to Mount Gilead, North Carolina. She always resented that move. When my father was not around, my mother bragged about her affair with a man named Kenneth and said he was very handsome and intelligent. She would then say, "I do not know how I ended up with a fool like your father." It appeared that she really loved Kenneth as he taught her how to survive in New York City.

I was always afraid to ask my mother why she named me Kenneth. Was it because of her extramarital affair with this man named Kenneth? Let's do the math. World War II ended in 1945. My father was discharged from the army immediately after the war. My parents spent two years in New York City and relocated to North Carolina in 1947. I was born in 1948. Makes me wonder, who is my daddy? I decided to just let it be as it was grown folks' business! I just wanted to stay off my mother's radar and avoid brutal beatings.

MY FATHER REHIRED BY ALCOA: ALCOA'S WORKING CONDITIONS

Not long after relocating from New York to Mount Gilead, North Carolina, my father was rehired by Alcoa Aluminum Company in Badin, North Carolina. He resumed his job as a blue-collar employee and worked in the extremely hot pot room. This was where iron ore was melted to make aluminum. Sometimes he received significant burns on his body after getting too close to the boiling pots. These hot pots emitted toxic gases. Decades later, it was alleged that black males who worked in the pot room had similar serious health problems because of inhaling toxic gases.

My father lost seniority with Alcoa as he did not return to work immediately after being discharged from the army in New York. He frequently blamed my mother's resistance to move back to Mount Gilead as the reason he lost seniority. Each workday, he drove his green manual-shift 1948 Chevrolet for thirty minutes from Mount Gilead to Badin, North Carolina. This car was massive in size and built like an army battle tank. In 1953, my father bought a new gray manual-shift Chevrolet.

CHAPTER 8

MY RHEUMATIC FEVER CONDITION

One day, my father drove my mother and me in his new Chevrolet from Mount Gilead, North Carolina, to Newport News, Virginia, to visit Grandfather and Grandmother Gould.

While visiting, at the age of five, I was stricken with rheumatic fever (heart condition) and was unable to walk. I had to use the strength in my arms and hands to drag my body across the floor. I was so afraid that I would never walk again. My mother telephoned her brother, Uncle Jacob, who also lived in Newport News, and explained my condition. Uncle Jacob and his wife, Aunt Laney, drove over immediately. Uncle Jacob picked me up in his arms, carried me to the car, and laid me down in the back seat. When we arrived at Doctor Williams' office, he carried me inside and I was seen by the doctor immediately. Doctor Williams prescribed medicine that helped me fully recover from rheumatic fever. I was thrilled to be able to walk and play again.

Unfortunately, after my recovery, my mother chastised me because it made her angry that I was not healthy like my first cousins

(Uncle Jacob and Aunt Laney's children). Her words had a negative impact on my self-esteem.

I thank God this childhood condition did not have future negative effects on my heart. My love for Uncle Jacob and Aunt Laney will forever be etched deeply in my heart.

MY LOVING DOG NAMED SKIP AND MY TRAUMATIC ACCIDENT

Although I experienced a lot of abuse from my mother in my young life, I was given a loving dog named Skip. He was my loving companion. Skip was just a puppy when a neighbor gave him to my father to groom as a rabbit-hunting dog. He was a small brown-and-white beagle puppy, and according to my father, Skip had no interest in chasing rabbits. Instead, Skip just wanted to run and play in the woods with me. We loved each other and were inseparable.

One day, during the dog days of August (hot, sultry days of summer), Skip and I were playing in the woods. I saw a hunter's animal trap and decided to pick it up. The trap closed quickly and almost cut off the middle finger on my right hand. Seeing me crying and bleeding, Skip ran to the house to get my mother.

Later, my mother told me Skip ran around on the front porch, barking loudly to get her attention. Skip then led my mother to me in the woods. When she arrived, I had removed my shirt and wrapped it around my finger that was dangling and bleeding profusely. Since my father was working, our white neighbor, named Ms. Daisy, drove me and my mother to see Dr. Ross. He cleaned my finger with alcohol and put in numerous stitches. I screamed loudly. Although my accident was traumatic, it was also a tender moment, as my parents showed affection toward me.

Several weeks later, my parents took me back to Dr. Ross for a follow-up visit. Dr. Ross told my parents, "Ken's finger is badly infected." He then said, "I may have to cut off his finger to prevent infection from spreading to other parts of his body." Hearing this, I jumped off the table and ran toward the door. My father caught me and brought me, kicking and screaming, back into the doctor's office. Dr. Ross cleaned my finger again with alcohol, wrapped it with a clean bandage, and increased my penicillin dosage. This treatment saved my finger.

CHAPTER 9

MY FAMILY MOVED FROM MOUNT GILEAD TO BADIN, NORTH CAROLINA

Before I started elementary school, my parents moved from Mount Gilead to Badin, North Carolina. Unfortunately, Skip somehow disappeared just before I moved away and was never seen again. My tears flowed profusely as I had lost my loving companion. Shortly thereafter, I felt Skip's loving spirit following me around in Badin. I talked, played, and embraced Skip's loving spirit. I felt Skip's presence embracing me especially when I was exposed to my mother's abuse. I was so happy to have him in my life again. To date, I believe Skip is still present in my life and continues to watch over and protect me.

I now have a beautiful tan Pomeranian dog named Prissy. She is my loving companion and follows me wherever I go. She even sleeps on the bedroom floor in her doggy bed right beneath my side of the bed. Friends call her the diva dog. She loves to pose to take pictures, loves going to doggy grooming, loves going to doggy day care to play with other dogs, loves sitting on my lap while I am watching TV, and loves riding in my arms when I am driving my car. I strongly believe Skip's loving spirit lives in Prissy.

MY PARENTS WANTED TO GIVE ME AWAY: INFORMAL ADOPTION

One summer day when I was six years old, my parents and I drove from Badin to Mount Gilead, North Carolina, to visit Grandfather and Grandmother Little and Aunt Ellen. Mrs. C. Seymour, a school teacher in Mount Gilead, stopped by the house to visit Aunt Ellen Little (my father's sister). Mrs. Seymour presented herself as an intelligent, very confident, and distinguished, well-groomed lady.

Aunt Ellen was a beautiful, light-brown-skinned tall woman with long black hair that bounced off her back when she walked. She was a gifted seamstress. Aunt Ellen's clients provided her with fabric and pictures of clothing from fashion magazines. She used her foot-operated sewing machine to make pictures become real for clients. If opportunities were available for Aunt Ellen in the early 1960s, models would have strolled down runways showcasing her fashions.

Mrs. Seymour purchased fabrics and brought it to Aunt Ellen to sew dresses and suits. During her visit with Aunt Ellen, she looked at me and told my parents, "I would love to have Kenneth as my little boy." To stop me from hearing their conversation, my parents made me go outside to play.

Suddenly, my parents drove thirty minutes to our house in Badin and came back with my clothes packed in a large brown paper bag. I then realized that they must have agreed to give me to

Mrs. Seymour. I wondered what their conversation was about while driving round-trip to get my clothes. I hit a dead end when I tried to figure out why they wanted to give me away.

Just as I was walking toward Mrs. Seymour's car, Grandfather and Grandmother Little intervened. They told my parents, "Do not give Ken away!" That day, Mrs. Seymour drove away with tears in her eyes. I cried too. This situation confirmed to me that my parents did not love me. Aside from my tears, I really wanted to go home with Mrs. Seymour to escape physical, verbal, and domestic abuse.

I also wondered why Mrs. Seymour was so concerned about my welfare. She continued her quest to make me her son by talking to Grandfather and Grandmother Little and Aunt Ellen. I am sure Aunt Ellen told her about the mental and physical abuse I experienced from my mother and distant relationship with my father. Aunt Ellen later told me that Mrs. Seymour constantly asked her if my parents had changed their minds about giving me away.

To date, I wonder if my mother's affair with Kenneth in New York City had caused my parents to consider giving me away.

REFORM SCHOOL THREAT (CURRENTLY KNOWN AS JUVENILE DETENTION)

My mother continually threatened to put me in reform school just to get rid of me. Reform school was for juvenile delinquents. I never committed a crime.

One day, while I was watching television, my mother walked into the living room and told me, "Pack your clothes in a large brown paper bag and go outside in the backyard and tell your father I said to take you to reform school in Cherokee, North Carolina."

I packed my clothes, went outside, and told my father, "Mama wants you to take me to reform school." Feeling frustrated, I told my father "I am ready to go to reform school!" At that young age, I was tired of my mother's erratic behavior.

My father glanced at me as he slowly pulled out one of his unfiltered Camel cigarettes and lit it. After a brief pause, he smiled and said, "Go back into the house and put your clothes away!" In a rare move, he stood up to my mother that day. He later encountered hours of cursing and screaming from her. Better him than me!

MY FATHER'S VERBAL BASHINGS

My mother gave my father daily verbal bashings. She continually tried to convince him that he was dumb and she was smart. She told him, "I am intellectually superior to you since I dropped out of school in the tenth grade and you dropped out in the eighth grade." She also contended, "I deserve an intelligent and sophisticated man for a husband."

He never responded to her rhetoric. He went outside for hours and worked in the vegetable garden and fed the pigs.

One day, I followed my father outside and stared at him with an inquisitive look on my face. He looked at me as though he was reading my mind and shared some words of wisdom. First, he said, "Boy, your mother cannot argue by herself—it takes two or more people to argue." Secondly, he said, "Has she ever packed her suitcase to leave?" He then chuckled and continued doing his chores.

CHAPTER 10

MY EARLY DEVELOPMENTAL YEARS

GROWING UP IN BADIN, NORTH CAROLINA

As noted earlier, my father was a blue-collar worker with Alcoa Aluminum Company. Alcoa was built in Badin in the early 1900s and used water from the Badin Lake to generate electricity for the company. In the 1950s, approximately 1,000 of 2,126 of the towns-people were employed by Alcoa. Most of them lived in company-owned houses.

The houses had white wood exteriors and similar interior floor plans. They also had screened-in front and back porches, with flushing toilets located on back porches. Further, kitchens had sinks and faucets with cold and hot running water. Bathrooms also had cold and hot running water that was used in sinks and four-legged French-style white bathtubs. Houses were heated with kerosene or coal-burning stoves. Life in the Alcoa housing was a great improvement over living in houses in Mount Gilead and other towns in North Carolina.

I was elated to live in a company-owned house in Badin.

There were boys my age to play with in the neighborhood. Initially, this felt like the ideal living situation for me.

Alcoa had excellent benefits and paid black male employees high wages for working in the hot pot room. The high wages afforded them opportunities to buy expensive cars and pickup trucks. Some employees built beautiful, new houses in or near Badin for their families. Black carpenters built most of these houses. Employees' family members were well-dressed and often attended socials to show off their fine wardrobes.

Most of the townspeople did not have formal education beyond high school, yet they encouraged their youth to attend college after graduating from high school. Most of the youth who graduated from college migrated to northern East Coast cities, such as Washington, DC; Baltimore, Maryland; Philadelphia, Pennsylvania; and New York City. They were in search of stable, good-paying white-collar or teaching jobs.

Even youth who did not attend college migrated to northern cities or joined the military in search of a different life. Most of them only returned to Badin for vacations or funerals, but never to live permanently. Overall, Badin was an affluent blue-collar town.

ADULTERY

Most blue-collar Alcoa employees, like my father, worked swing shift schedules (7:00 a.m. to 3:00 p.m., 3:00 p.m. to 11:00 p.m. or 11:00 p.m. to 7:00 a.m.). These work schedules paved the way for a lot of adultery.

It was town gossip that my mother developed her mental condition shortly after I was born. Was there a connection between my mother's pregnancy and postpartum depressions? If there was, her mental condition was left untreated.

Although my mother did not have a job, men gave her money

and bought her expensive clothes and shoes at high-end, fashionable department stores. These stores were in Salisbury, North Carolina, twenty-three miles from Badin. Some of the men who dated my mother grew up with my father or became his so-called friends at Alcoa. In fact, my mother would drive my father's 1953 Chevrolet down old country dirt roads in the woods to reward men with sex. From a layman's point of view, this behavior confirmed her bipolar mental health condition.

During her sexual encounters, she made me get out and walk away from the car. Each time, it was within earshot, and tears would stream down my young face. I could hear her moaning, and I could see the car rapidly bouncing up and down while she was having sex.

After her escapade was over, my mother would say, "Get back into the car." An unpleasant odor of sex, cigarette smoke, and liquor lingered inside the car. As we drove along, I pretended to be playing and put my head out of the car window to inhale fresh air. She consistently threatened me by saying, "I will beat your ass if you tell your father!"

She would then stop at a roadside country store to buy me a hot dog and a soft drink. This was a regular reward for me not to mention her secret affairs to my father. I felt like I was betraying my father by not telling him about my mother's behavior. However, I knew she would not spare the rod on my behind if I told him. So, I kept quiet.

There was also mean-spirited town gossip floating around Badin that I was conceived during one of my mother's extramarital affairs. It was obvious that parents discussed my mother's behavior in front of my childhood friends. They often teased me about my mother's mental health condition and sexual behavior. Most of these parents committed adultery too. The adage "If you live in a glass house, do not throw stones" applies here. Their parents lived in glass houses. I felt hopeless, as there were no adults I could confide in regarding this situation.

One evening, two of my playmates, named Jerry and Mike, quietly climbed an apple tree to steal some apples at John the Bootlegger's house. While in the tree, they peeped through the window and saw my mother and John having sex on the floor. The next day, when they saw me, they laughed and yelled, "We saw your mother. She was drunk and having sex with John the Bootlegger." They teased me all day, and I felt so helpless. Happiness for me then was just an illusion.

MY FATHER'S REPUTATION VERSUS MY MOTHER'S

As far back as I can remember, no parents or children ever teased me about my father's behavior or him having an extramarital affair. The townspeople always made positive comments about my hard-working, responsible father. Strangely enough, he was committed to my mother and was an excellent provider. He held on tightly to his money and was not a frivolous spender. If a person looked up the word frugal in the dictionary, my father's picture would appear right beside the definition. He always paid his bills and saved money for a rainy day. Because he did not trust banks, he saved his money under lock and key in his old Army footlocker.

Conversely, my mother was completely opposite my father. She was unemployed, flamboyant, loved money, and bought expensive clothes and shoes to wear in public to seduce men and make women jealous. On several occasions, my mother stole money from my father's footlocker. He cursed at her for a little while then retreated to his bedroom.

On a typical day, especially when my father was at work,

my mother spent most of her time drinking liquor in bootleggers' houses, visiting people who tolerated her erratic behavior or staying at home in bed.

MY MOTHER'S GANGSTER GIRLFRIEND

One day, my mother's girlfriend, Mrs. Razor, stopped by the house for a visit. Mrs. Razor had a notorious reputation for cutting people with her barber's razor. She always carried the razor inside her bra. My father later joined them at the kitchen table to have a few drinks of moonshine white liquor.

Mrs. Razor and my mother were really intoxicated. Suddenly, Mrs. Razor turned to my mother and said, "You should be ashamed of yourself for treating your husband like you do. I wish I had this handsome, hardworking man!" I guess the old folk tale is true; "a drunken person speaks a sober person's mind." The liquor made her confess suppressed romantic fantasies she had about my father.

Songwriters wrote powerful lyrics that said, "They're smiling in your face and all the time they want to take your place—they're back-stabbers!" Mrs. Razor's confession about her affection for my father really rocked my mother's world. My mother politely asked her to leave the house. This polite behavior was highly unusual for my mother. Obviously, she feared Mrs. Razor would reach inside her bra and pull out the razor to cut her. After she left, my father looked at my mother and laughed out of control. Eventually, he got up from the table and went outside and worked in his vegetable garden to escape my mother's verbal abuse.

CHASTISED ABOUT MY HEALTH PROBLEMS

As noted earlier, I was extremely underweight during early childhood and experienced numerous health problems. My mother chastised me by saying, "I don't know why you are not healthy like other children your age!" I thought to myself, If other children lived with you, they would be unhealthy too. This thought made me very nervous as I thought she could read my mind! My mother's cold, hard stare made my whole-body tremble.

I frequently wore an angry look that seemed to be etched deeply into my face. When I attended church Sunday school classes, I prayed for God to stop anger from penetrating my soul. I also prayed that my father would stay at peace when hearing mean town gossip.

CHAPTER 11

MY MOTHER'S LOVER

My father knew one of my mother's lovers who was a blue-collar worker at Alcoa and a key church official, named Mr. Pimp. One morning, I was awakened to sounds of birds chirping and the neighbors' dogs barking. The fresh, sweet smell of wild honeysuckle flowers filled the air.

As I crawled out of bed, I noticed a trail of blood on the floor leading to the front door. I then saw a pair of bloodstained alligator high-heeled shoes on the floor near the front door. This really startled me. I walked into my parents' bedroom and asked my father, "Where is Mama? And why is there blood on the floor beside Mama's shoes?"

My father replied, "I don't know. And stop asking so many questions." He then told me to go into the kitchen, get a bowl of cornflakes, and not use too much sugar.

Later that morning, my mother's cousin Diane stopped by the house to talk to my father. She lived in an Alcoa-owned house several blocks from us. I overheard her asking my father if my mother could come back home. My father raised his voice and said, "I am tired of her stuff. I saw her kissing Mr. Pimp on the back porch at the bootlegger's house last night!"

Mr. Pimp was a member at the same church my mother and I attended. Since my mother did not have a lot of money, my father concluded Mr. Pimp bought the expensive alligator shoes for my mother. My father used the shoes to beat my mother.

My father later allowed me to walk with cousin Diane to her house to see my mother. I started crying when I saw my mother's battered and bruised face and head. A few days later, my father allowed my mother to come back home.

After my mother's injuries healed, she continued her romance with Mr. Pimp. She made me carry written notes to him at church. The notes listed a time and place they could meet in the woods. He always gave me fifty cents when I delivered my mother's notes.

On these Sundays, I ended up with seventy-five cents in my pocket. I got fifty cents from Mr. Pimp and kept the twenty-five cents I was supposed to put in the church's collection plate. I learned that trick by watching older boys in church. They hit the bottom of the collection plate to make the sound of putting coins in the plate. I used this trick to keep my money too.

My Sunday school teacher eventually caught me and threatened to tell my parents. However, she never did, because she knew my mother would give me a savage beating.

Mr. Pimp was arrogant and chased a lot of women in church, in neighborhoods, and in neighboring communities. I did not like him. He had several children outside his marriage and was not a positive role model.

Mr. Pimp and my mother played a crazy game of "who's zooming whom?" They had lots of affairs with other people. However, their affair was like junkies with crack cocaine addictions. They were addicted to each other! My father repeatedly physically battered my mother because of her extramarital affair with Mr.

Pimp.

My father's behavior made me angry with him. There were times when I jumped on his back crying and begging him to stop beating my mother, but despite my father's physical abuse, my mother continued dating Mr. Pimp and other men.

MR. PIMP'S WIFE'S CAR CHASE WITH MY MOTHER

One day, my mother and I were driving through Badin. Mrs. Pimp suddenly appeared and started chasing my mother with her car.

They were speeding through Badin's very narrow streets. I was afraid as I was sitting in the front seat during the chase. I cried and braced myself by putting my hands on the car's dashboard.

Suddenly, my mother slowed the car down, jumped out, and ran into Mrs. Razor's house. The car was still moving in slow motion when I moved into the driver's seat to hit the brakes to stop the car. I then applied the emergency brakes.

Mrs. Razor came out of her house to get me out of the car. She then reached into her bra and pulled out her barber's razor and told Mrs. Pimp to go home or else. She drove away quietly as she was keenly aware of Mrs. Razor's reputation for cutting people with her razor.

My mother and Mrs. Razor made amends that day. My mother never truly forgave her for flirting with my father, as she continually badgered my father about that situation. However, my mother and Mrs. Razor moved forward, going on double dates again, meeting men in the woods and having sex. I felt so bad for my father.

TOXIC RELATIONSHIPS

After experiencing my parents' abusive behavior toward each other, I learned a life lesson. I concluded that if a spouse is involved in an extramarital affair, it is a toxic relationship. Physical and emotional abuse will not stop a spouse from participating in an extramarital affair. He or she will ultimately devise clever ways to continue the affair.

Further, from a personal perspective, I believe parents' negative behavior in front of children eventually creates psychological scars and future cycles of dysfunctional behavior. Staying in a marriage for the sake of children can sometimes be counterproductive. Couples should explore individual, family, and marital counseling as possible healing options. Sometimes divorce is inevitable but should be the last resort for married couples.

MY FAMILY'S SURVIVOR TECHNIQUES DURING HARD TIMES

My father was a quiet, hard-working man and an excellent provider. When aluminum sales were slow, Alcoa laid off numerous employees. To ensure we always had sufficient food, my father rented property from a neighbor and planted a large vegetable garden. The garden contained early June peas, turnip greens, white and sweet potatoes, okra, tomatoes, corn, beets, watermelons, cantaloupes, and more. In the late spring and early summer, the family worked together to harvest and prepare vegetables for storage.

Selected vegetables were steamed in large pots of boiling water. Next step, half-gallon mason jars were washed by hand in hot, soapy water and subsequently boiled in a large pot to ensure food safety. The steamed vegetables were then placed in half-gallon mason jars with jar tops tightly sealed by hand. After the jars cooled, they were stored at room temperature in a dark room. Other steamed vegetables were placed in large plastic freezer bags and stored in the family's large white deep freezer. All stored vegetables had a fresh taste when cooked and were served for dinner in winter months.

The family also harvested, canned, and stored fruit (blackberries, apples, peaches, and pears) in mason jars and large freezer bags and stored in the freezer. My parents cooked some of the fruit and made homemade fruit jellies and jams.

The family also went fishing at nearby ponds and lakes and caught numerous fish, such as catfish, carp, perch, and more. After we cleaned the fish, they were placed in large freezer bags and stored in the large white deep freezer.

During late fall and winter, my father hunted wild game such as rabbits, raccoons, and squirrels. They were cleaned and stored in the freezer.

Only when necessary, we went to the grocery store to buy a twenty-five-pound bag of flour, milk, and a large bucket of lard (shortening) to make biscuits. Life lesson: my parents often said, we must live like squirrels, because they store nuts and acorns away during the summer and fall to have food to eat during winter.

CHAPTER 12

WEST BADIN'S ECONOMY

West Badin had black-owned businesses, which enabled the community to be self-sufficient. There were numerous black churches, two barbershops, local grocery stores, and a gas station. There were two main entertainment facilities. One was a pool hall equipped with pool tables, a music jukebox, and a large dance floor. The owner sold snacks and soft drinks to customers. The other was a very clean café that sold delicious dinners, sandwiches, and soft drinks. It also had a music jukebox with the latest songs for customers to sing along and dance to.

WEST BADIN'S BOOTLEGGERS

There were numerous West Badin bootleggers who sold illegal moonshine liquor, beer, and sealed liquor. When customers asked bootleggers for "sealed liquor," they wanted liquor bootleggers purchased from State-owned legal alcohol beverage controlled (ABC) stores. Customers ordered liquor by asking for a fifty-cent shot, a dollar shot, and on up to a pint, quart, or half-gallon in mason jars. They identified liquor they wanted to drink by asking for white or brown liquor. White liquor included moonshine, gin, rum, or vodka. Brown liquor was scotch, bourbon, and others.

ABC stores paid taxes on liquor sales and were in commonly known "wet" counties. Stanly County, at that time, where West Badin is located, was a "dry" county. This meant selling alcoholic beverages in West Badin was illegal.

ACROSS BADIN'S RAILROAD TRACK

White people lived across the railroad track in segregated Badin. Businesses located in Badin included Alcoa, a segregated doctor's office, a segregated movie theater, segregated restaurants, a segregated eighteen-hole golf course, a drugstore, gas stations, and the local post office. It was common practice for businesses to close at 12:00 p.m. every Wednesday and stay open until 12:00 p.m. every Saturday.

Black people had to sit in a separate room from white people at the doctor's office. Black moviegoers had to sit upstairs in movie theaters while white moviegoers sat on the first floor, where refreshments were located. At segregated restaurants, blacks entered through a back door labeled colored only to order food. They were not allowed to eat food in the white only part of the restaurant.

Blacks were strictly prohibited from playing golf on the eighteen-hole segregated golf course. Young black caddies refined their golfing skills by playing golf on holes surrounded by woods. When the lookout person (young black person) saw white golfers approaching the area, everyone would run and hide in the woods.

BADIN'S GARBAGE DUMP

Garbage collected from West Badin and Badin was dumped

in the West Badin community. On rainy, hot, windy days in the summer, odor from the massive garbage dump was horrific. It smelled like an open-air raw sewage plant and was also an eyesore to the West Badin community. Protests from West Badin citizens eventually closed the garbage dump.

CHAPTER 13

MY EDUCATION JOURNEY AND EXPERIENCES IN BADIN, NORTH CAROLINA

PRESCHOOL VACCINATIONS

The law required all students entering school to receive a series of vaccinations for measles, mumps, polio, and others. My parents took me to West Badin School for vaccinations. All incoming first graders in August 1954 formed a single line along the wall leading to Principal Black's office. I was happy playing with my future classmates while we moved along the wall. Then it was my turn to receive my vaccinations.

At first glance, I noticed the principal's office had a large brown wooden desk, a large leather chair, and was cluttered with books, stacks of papers, and manual typewriters.

Later, I noticed a petite white lady with light-colored hair. She was wearing a starched white dress with a black-and-white name tag on it. The name tag had her name on it and RN (registered nurse). I heard my parents speak and call her Nurse Foster. She was also wearing a starched white hat that was placed neatly on top of her light-colored hair, along with white stockings and clean white shoes.

Nurse Foster looked scary standing there holding several needles in hand. She smiled and motioned for me to come into the principal's office. The office had a smell of alcohol that permeated the air and made me feel dizzy.

Suddenly, I started having heart palpitations and a panic attack inside my head. This setting made me have a flashback to a year ago, when my parents took me into the doctor's office in Mount Gilead after I sustained a deep cut on the middle finger of my right hand. I ran out of the doctor's office that day, and my father ran me down and brought me back for treatment.

Well, history repeated itself. I ran out of the principal's office. I ran fast, heading straight toward the school's exit door. My father ran me down again and brought me back into the principal's office to get my vaccinations. I was so afraid I could see my heart pounding through my shirt. My father held my arms and legs while Nurse Foster gave me vaccinations. I had a bunch of curse words in my head but was afraid to say them out loud. My shirt was soaking wet from my watershed of tears. I was one angry little skinny boy that day.

MY EDUCATION JOURNEY

I have documented my education journey for selected grades at the West Badin School in Badin, North Carolina.

The school was built in the early 1900s. When I entered the first grade in 1954, the school's physical structure was a three-story redbrick building. A combined gymnasium and auditorium and several classrooms were located upstairs on the third floor. The school's main entrance was on the ground level. The office of Mr. Black, the school principal, and most classrooms were also located on this level. The cafeteria, storage rooms, restrooms, and a large coal-burning furnace to heat the school were in the basement. The school was renovated in the 1960s. A new gymnasium, auditorium, cafeteria, and wing of classrooms were built.

West Badin School was a segregated school located in a segregated community. West was the term used to identify the black community of Badin. West Badin School had a total student enrollment of around 450, which included elementary, middle, and high school students.

Mr. Black and the teachers were black and highly educated and motivated to teach black students. School spirit was extremely high and was strongly supported by students and parents. The spirited marching band and melodic choir performed beautiful music. The football and basketball teams had numerous winning seasons.

There were some pivotal moments in West Badin School's history. Although West Badin's student body was small and part of a small segregated athletic division, the boys' basketball team defeated 4A division schools (large student bodies in urban cities) to win state championships. During these times, the school's spirit exploded on campus and throughout West Badin. To date, these championships are still a source of pride for former West Badin School students and townspeople.

MY FIRST DAY OF SCHOOL

On the first day of school, my arms were still sore from the vaccinations. My mother dressed me in a matching short pants and shirt and a new pair of PF Flyers tennis shoes. I really wanted an expensive pair of All-Star Converse tennis shoes. Because my feet were still growing and the tennis shoes were expensive, my parents refused to buy them.

As I crossed the street, two high school girls walking down the sidewalk started laughing and teasing me and said, "Look at his skinny legs!" I did not know their names. Because I had fragile feelings and low self-esteem, I started crying and ran back home. After observing me for a few minutes, my mother agreed to let me put on a pair of long pants. She must have been in a good mood that day. She did not make me wear shorts to school again.

One afternoon, while walking home from school, I heard several high school boys making vulgar remarks about one another's mother. I decided to copy their behavior. Eventually, I saw the two girls who had previously teased me, and I made a bold move. I told them, "Your mama loves rubbing my skinny legs and this, too." I grabbed my crouch then.

One girl said, "Little boy, I will spank your butt and tell your mother I did it!"

The other girl told her friend, "Girl, you better leave him alone, because his mother is crazy."

Getting even with these girls made me feel good. I laughed and ran home. They never bothered me again.

COUNTY SCHOOL BOARD

When the county school board (white members only) purchased new schoolbooks, most of the new books were given to white schools. Used books were shipped from Badin schools to West Badin. One day, when my teacher gave me schoolbooks for the year, I saw the surname Honeycutt written on the book's inside cover. A white student with the surname Honeycutt was the last student to use the book. No one in West Badin had the surname of Honeycutt.

This did not impede the education process in West Badin. Again, Mr. Black and other teachers were motivated to teach West Badin students. No student was left behind.

FIRST GRADE, 1954

My first-grade teacher's name was Mrs. Dawkins. In addition to teaching first grade, she taught music and directed the school band. We played instruments such as cymbals, drums, and bells daily in her class. Mrs. Dawkins directed the class as we banged out noise with instruments. If she caught us not paying attention, she would hit us across our knuckles with a drumstick. I never got hit with the drumstick as I paid attention in class. Besides, seeing my classmates get hit with the drumstick and crying motivated me to pay attention.

I really loved playing and listening to music. One day, Mrs. Dawkins surprised the class and brought her son to school. He is now a legendary recording artist. She used a portable record player to play one of his new songs at that time. I really embraced music more than other school subjects.

We also had to recite poetry in class. I remember this funny poem: "Girls are made of sugar and spice and everything nice. Boys are made of snakes and snails and puppy dog tails." For some unknown reason, I loved this poem.

One day, Mrs. Dawkins told me to give my mother this sealed note. My heart was pounding, and my brain was racing trying to figure out what I had done wrong. My hands were shaking as I gave my mother the note. She read the note and started cursing. I was really terrified and so afraid of getting a brutal beating. She then told me Mrs. Dawkins wrote in her note that my first name should be spelled "Kennith" and not "Kenneth." I was so relieved the note was not about my behavior in school.

I was caught in the middle of their argument as I carried notes back and forth for at least a week. Finally, one day, without notice, Mrs. Dawkins stopped by our house to discuss my name issue with my mother. While hiding under the bed, I heard Mrs. Dawkins tell my mother, "Going forward, I will accept 'Kenneth' as the proper spelling of his name."

My mother told her, "His name was printed as 'Kenneth' in the family Bible. This was done on the same day the midwife delivered him in our old country house in Mount Gilead, North Carolina."

My parents used the Bible as proof to secure my official birth certificate at the Montgomery County Courthouse in Troy, North Carolina. This was a common practice in rural towns in North Carolina. Although the issue was resolved, I was embarrassed and never felt comfortable again in Mrs. Dawkins's class.

I was promoted to the second grade in 1955.

CHAPTER 14

SUMMER VACATION WITH GRANDFATHER AND GRANDMOTHER LITTLE

That summer, I was eight years old. I started spending summers with my loving grandparents Grandfather and Grandmother Little and Aunt Ellen. They lived in a sharecropper house in Mount Gilead, North Carolina. One day, I was walking around the house without a shirt on, and Grandmother Little asked, "How did you get those deep scars on your back?" She then fetched a bottle of white-colored ointment and lovingly rubbed it on my bruised back.

I begged her not to mention it to anyone and reluctantly told her my mother beat me with a dogwood tree branch because I caused her to have a nervous breakdown. I was often forced to make several trips into the woods before my mother was satisfied with the size and length of the tree branch.

Grandmother Little did not comment on my response; she just frowned and mumbled some words under her breath. She then clearly stated, "God help this child!"

LITTLE FAMILY HISTORY

I loved staying with Grandfather and Grandmother Little and Aunt Ellen during the summer. Grandfather Little was a tall, dark-skinned, robust man. He enjoyed being a farmer. One day, Grandfather Little told me, "I was in my early twenties when your grandmother was born." After he saw how pretty she was as a baby, he said, "I put the word out right then in the local community that when she is old enough, I am going to marry her." Grandfather Little married Grandmother Little when she was thirteen years old. They produced five boys and one girl. My father was the eldest child.

My great-grandmother McRae was a dark-skinned slave. Grandmother Little's father was a white plantation slave owner. This slave owner also had another daughter with my great-grandmother McRae's sister, who was also a dark-skinned slave. My great-aunt's name was Katherine. It appeared the white slave owner raped both slave sisters.

One afternoon, Grandmother Little and Aunt Katherine were sitting beside each other on the front porch. I commented, "Both of you look like sisters." It was just my friendly observation, or so I thought. They just stared at me. They had very fair skin complexion, keen facial features like white people, and long black hair. They looked like identical twins.

Eventually, Grandmother Little, who uncommonly raised her voice, shouted, "Stay out of grown folks' business, boy!" I never interfered in that situation again.

GOING FISHING WITH GRANDMOTHER LITTLE

I loved going fishing with Grandmother Little on selected Saturdays. We walked three miles to fish in the Big River. As we walked toward the river, Grandmother Little always shared life lessons with me. She told me, "Do not dislike mean people, and always honor and respect your parents regardless of the situation." Secretly, in my heart and mind, I wanted to reject my grandmother's wisdom regarding my parents.

During these walks, she always had her bottom lip full of Old Navy snuff (finely ground dark-brown-colored tobacco powder). One day, I asked her, "Why do you dip snuff?" Her response was "Because I am grown and it tastes good to me and you are too young to use tobacco products."

While at the river, I was searching through her fishing tackle bag and found her can of Old Navy snuff. I disobeyed my grandmother and put a large dip of snuff in my bottom lip. It tasted awful! Minutes later, I felt dizzy and started throwing up. She fussed at me for a few minutes for disobeying her. She then laughed and said, "You are one stubborn boy. I hope you learned your lesson."

GRANDMOTHER LITTLE'S SECRET FISHING BAIT

My grandmother had a secret recipe for making fish bait for catching huge carp (bottom-feeding fish) in the Big River. Hiding and observing my grandmother, I saw her mixing flour and water to make thick dough. She then added cotton balls to hold the dough together. Lastly, she added vanilla flavor to appeal to carp's keen sense of smell.

GRANDMOTHER LITTLE'S FISHING TECHNIQUES

My grandmother cut down large bamboo to use as a fishing pole. She told me bamboo was one of the strongest woods in the world. She repeatedly wrapped course fishing line around the fishing pole. She then attached heavy weights to make the large steel hook and bait sink deep into the bottom of the river.

She would then throw kernels of corn in the fishing area to attract a group of carp to her fishing hole. This enabled her to catch huge carp (yellow- or blue-scaled carp). When Grandmother Little caught a huge carp, she shared it with neighbors.

MY SATURDAY CAR RIDES WITH GRANDFATHER LITTLE

Another exciting adventure I experienced during the summer was car rides with Grandfather Little on selected Saturdays—just the two of us. He advised me on life issues. He constantly reminded me to be a responsible man, save money for a rainy day, go to college to get an education, get a good-paying white-collar job, get married to a loving and supportive wife and buy property and a house. He further advised me to have children and teach them the same life values and responsibilities.

Sometimes I felt like I was too young to understand and retain the wisdom my grandfather was imparting, but I did retain most of it. My grandfather greatly influenced my dreams and visions.

SUNDAY MORNINGS IN THE COUNTRY: MOUNT GILEAD, NORTH CAROLINA

On Sunday mornings, I waited for Grandmother Little's big red rooster to crow. The rooster's loud crow served as the alarm clock to wake the Little family each morning. The rooster's other chore was to fertilize female chickens (hens).

The rooster's crow was my signal to get out of bed and go into the kitchen to make a fire in the wood-stove. My grandmother taught me how to pour kerosene on wood in the stove to start the fire. I threw a lighted match onto the wood and jumped back to avoid getting burned. I would then go back to bed.

I was awakened by the pleasant aroma of fried fish, homemade yellow grits, fried eggs, and hot butter-tasting biscuits. The food's aroma flowed through the air from the kitchen into the bedroom. The food was so delicious it stirred my taste buds and danced on my tongue. I could taste love in the food!

GETTING DRESSED FOR ALL-DAY CHURCH SERVICE

After eating a hearty breakfast on Sunday, I helped clean the dishes. My next chore was to put more wood in the stove to keep the fire burning to heat water for each family member to take a bath. I made numerous trips with a water bucket to and from the hand-operated pump in the backyard to retrieve water. I filled several washtubs with hot water for bathing. The family used homemade lye soap to clean their bodies. The soap really left a dirty ring around the washtub.

When everyone was dressed in their Sunday clothes, we started the four-mile walk to church. Since Grandfather Little was superintendent of the Baptist Church, he drove the car to church early to clean up and get organized for morning and afternoon services. We stayed all day for Sunday church services.

TWO CHURCHES AND THE LITTLE FAMILY CEMETERY IN MOUNT GILEAD, NORTH CAROLINA

Two churches were located across a dirt road from each other, both within walking distance of each other. One church was Baptist, and the other was Methodist. Both congregations alternated having church services, one Sunday at the Baptist Church and the other Sunday at the Methodist Church.

There was also a large cemetery located in the woods behind both churches. Little family members who were plantation slaves and generations of Little family members thereafter are buried in the cemetery. Local and family members who migrated to northern cities are buried there, as grave plots are free.

Grandfather Little was around eighty-three years old and Grandmother Little was around seventy-six when they passed away. Their deaths left a gigantic hole in my mind, heart, and soul. Both of my grandparents passed away in the 1970s.

While I'm sitting at my computer, writing about my grandparents, loving memories of them cause my tears to flow profusely like a river during a heavy rainstorm. These are tears of joy! I am just overwhelmed with fond memories and how I was blessed to have such loving grandparents. I know God is blessing them in heaven. Nothing in this world can match grandparents' love. I feel lost and all alone since they are not here on earth anymore, continuing to share their beautiful love with me. I know they are watching over me in heaven. I celebrate their love.

Grandfather and Grandmother Little, my father and mother, and Aunt Ellen are buried in the Little cemetery.

DEATH OF MY PARENTS

My mother was sixty-one years old when she died from two concurrent massive strokes. During our last visit at the hospital, the doctor informed us that she was brain dead. My father looked at me and said, "She is your mother. You make the final decision to take her off life support." My father turned and walked away. I gave the doctor consent to take her off life support.

In my mind, my mother's strokes could have possibly been prevented if she had sought regular care from a medical doctor. My father's medical insurance at Alcoa would have covered her medical expenses. She viewed medical doctors as thieves who just wanted to take her money. Instead, she chose to self-diagnose her conditions. When I became ill, she would concoct a strange dose of bitter-tasting herbs and make me swallow it. The potion burned starting with my tongue and all the way down to my stomach. I was too afraid to ask her the name of her homemade concoction.

My mother went to witchcraft workers and went into the woods to dig up roots for treatment. That was her fatal mistake. Besides, when she died, she left around $1,400 in credit card debt for my father to pay. My father was totally unaware that she used credit cards. She had forged his name on credit card applications. He also had to pay cash for her burial expenses that totaled around $5,000.

My father told me to spend as little money as possible for my mother's burial because she did not have life insurance. He also said out of spite that my mother would not sign Alcoa's life insurance policy because she did not want my father to receive any insurance money. My mother always boasted that she would live longer than my father. Obviously, that was another one of my mother's fatal mistakes.

MY MOTHER'S FUNERAL

My mother's funeral was in Badin, North Carolina. It was at the same church where my mother and I were members. It was also the church where her deceased lover, Mr. Pimp, was a member. During the pastor's eulogy for my mother, he mentioned, "I eulogized Mr. Pimp one year ago almost to the day." When the pastor mentioned the late Mr. Pimp, whether intentionally or unintentionally, his words cut into me and my father like a knife. It was so strange—the pastor had a stroke in the pulpit after referring to Mr. Pimp at my mother's funeral. Mr. Pimp still haunted my father, even from the grave.

Grandfather Gould, now over the age of eighty, was very distraught at my mother's funeral. He repeatedly cried out loud, "I have lost my baby! A parent is not supposed to bury his child. I lost my wife, and now I have lost my daughter."

Grandmother Gould was around eighty years old when she died in the late 1970s. This was over a decade before my mother's death. My mother claimed to be too sick to attend Grandmother Gould's funeral. Grandfather Gould was ninety-five years old when he passed away in the mid-1990s. Uncle Jacob was the last person left of the family of four. He passed away around 2012 at the age of ninety-two.

Although my mother hated the Little family, my father insisted that we bury her in the Little cemetery. He was adamant that we not spend a lot of money to bury her. I never challenged him on the issue. I was keenly aware of his anger toward my mother.

My father eventually met a young lady named Julie and fell deeply in love with her. One day, he told me, "Boy, I never knew a woman could treat me so nice." I was happy that my father finally enjoyed love and peace in his lifetime.

My father passed away at the age of sixty-eight. It was roughly eighteen months after my mother's death. My father died from terminal lung cancer that might have evolved from two sources. First, he smoked a pack of unfiltered Camel cigarettes each day for years. Secondly, his death might have allegedly been caused by inhaling dangerous gas fumes while working in Alcoa's pot room for over thirty years.

A lot of Little family secrets are buried in the Little cemetery. Unfortunately, I still don't know why my mother blamed me for her nervous breakdown. The same is true for my father; he passed before explaining why he maintained a distant relationship with me.

SUNDAY CHURCH SERVICE

During Sunday church service, I always sat very close to Grandmother Little, except when she played the piano to accompany the congregation singing heartfelt spirituals. The louder the congregation sang, the harder Grandmother Little banged on the old piano.

Although my grandmother did not play the piano that well, I always complimented her by saying, "You played beautiful music on the piano today!" She always smiled and said, "Thank you, baby!" One day, I asked her, "How did you learn to play the piano?" She said, "I never had piano lessons. I just let the Holy Spirit guide me."

One Sunday while we were in church, my grandmother started crying, jumping, and shouting. Her actions really caught me by surprise. I started crying too and wondered what was wrong with my grandmother. Out of concern, when she calmed down, I asked her, "Why were you crying so hard?"

She said, "You will understand when you are older."

Life lesson: my life's trials and tribulations taught me what she meant that Sunday.

I love and miss Grandmother Little!

The old church was very hot in the summer, especially when the congregation felt the Holy Spirit and started crying, jumping, and shouting. When church members fainted, they were shown love, support, and understanding. Paper fans were used to keep members cool, and they were given natural spring water to drink. They used a water bucket to get water from the natural spring located in a wooded area down the hill behind the Baptist Church. Recycled twelve-ounce tin cans that once contained vegetables were used as drinking cups.

SUNDAY EVENINGS
AFTER CHURCH SERVICE

After church, the family rode home in Grandfather Little's car. Grandmother Little and Aunt Ellen prepared delicious Sunday dinners and desserts. They prepared macaroni loaded with sharp cheddar cheese, golden-brown fried chicken, fresh, just picked from the-garden green cabbage seasoned with chopped bits of sugar-cured ham, freshly churned buttermilk, butter-flavored corn muffins, grape-flavored Kool-Aid, yellow cake with chocolate icing, and blackberry pie. When I walked into the kitchen, the aroma of the food just lifted me off the floor! After dinner dishes were cleaned, the family retired to the front porch to laugh, talk, and relax.

When gnats and mosquitoes swarmed around the porch, Grandfather Little sent me inside the house to get a large bucket, newspaper, old clothes, and matches so he could start a fire. Smoke from the fire chased the gnats and mosquitoes away.

MILKING THE COW AND MAKING HOMEMADE DAIRY PRODUCTS

Grandmother Little also taught me how to milk the cow. Her name was Daisy. Late in the evenings, we washed Daisy's milk bag and tits to avoid getting waste in the milk bucket. During my first try, I squeezed Daisy's tits too hard. She kicked me in the stomach, and I landed in a pile of Daisy's waste.

After observing that I was okay, my grandmother laughed at me. She made me get up and go to the pump and wash off Daisy's waste. Against my wishes, she made me try milking Daisy again. This time, I was gentle with Daisy, and milk flowed into the bucket. My next chore was to pour the fresh milk into a churn located in the kitchen.

CHURNING DAISY'S FRESH MILK TO MAKE BUTTER & BUTTERMILK

The churn was made of hard clay and shaped like a bullet. The lid had a one-inch hole in the center to prevent milk from splashing on the floor. The wooden handle was three feet long and was inserted in the center of the clay lid. The handle's bottom had five three-inch wooden prongs that rested at the bottom of the churn.

With my hands, I manually moved the handle in a constant up-and-down motion. This constant motion and wooden prongs at the bottom of the churn eventually caused the milk to form butter. This manual churning took about forty-five minutes to an hour. It was a tiring process as I had to constantly change hands to complete the task. The fresh butter gave hot biscuits, corn bread, and other foods a rich-tasting flavor. We drank fresh buttermilk with meals.

GRANDMOTHER LITTLE'S OLD FASHIONED LAUNDRY TECHNIQUES

On rainy days, Grandmother Little showed me how to place washtubs and barrels under the house's downspouts to catch rainwater. She told me, "God's pure rainwater makes bed linen really white and clean."

She started a fire under a large black iron washpot to boil the rainwater. She later added homemade lye soap and placed bed linens in the boiling rainwater. With her method, the bed linen was white as snow, hanging on outdoor clotheslines and blowing in the summer breeze.

LITTLE FAMILY'S SUMMER PARTIES

Each summer, the Little family members would drive down from northern states to visit Grandfather and Grandmother Little and Aunt Ellen. The house was full of family members. Adults slept in beds, and children slept on the floor on pallets (handmade quilts doubled up for cushion).

Women family members cooked for hours on the wood-stove to prepare delicious food and desserts such as cakes and pies, Jell-O, biscuits, rice, and banana puddings. The kitchen was extremely hot. The rotating electric fan only circulated hot air in the kitchen.

Everyone had beverages to drink with their meal. Using cold water and ice from the refrigerator, adults made grape or strawberry flavored Kool-Aid for children to drink. Adults drank various flavors of bottled sodas or alcoholic beverages. Adult beverages were stored in a large washtub with a large chunk of ice. Another large washtub was full of ice-cold watermelons that we picked from Grandmother Little's garden.

Since Grandfather Little was the superintendent of the church, he told everyone he had to abstain from drinking alcohol. It was always fun watching Grandfather Little hang out around the large washtub that was full of ice-cold beer. Grandfather Little would sneak two cans of beer out of the tub, wrap them in newspaper, and retreat to the outdoor toilet to drink them. After several trips to the toilet, he was intoxicated. He would get loud and start telling jokes. Family members laughed and joked about Grandfather Little being intoxicated. This was done quietly behind his back.

The atmosphere at family functions was filled with love. I truly miss the memorable, fun-filled family functions. More importantly, I still love and miss Grandfather and Grandmother Little.

CHAPTER 15

MY FIRST PAYING JOB

During the summer, when I was eight, Grandfather Little got me my first paying job. I started as water boy, earning $2 per day. I carried water for the white overseer (supervisor) named Mr. Manson and black cotton fieldworkers to drink. The rows of grassy cotton seemed to be a mile long in hot, sandy cotton fields. Black people chopped the grass away from rows of cotton.

I walked a mile each way on an old dirt road to retrieve drinking water in a large clear glass jug. My short pants, T-shirt, and caramel-colored straw hat were soaking wet with sweat after each trip I made to the hand-operated water pump. When I walked along the dirt road, I was on high alert due to seeing poisonous snakes crawling around and other wild animals making loud noises in the woods. I often saw deer, rabbits, and squirrels playing in the woods. I was terrified of potentially encountering a bear or fox, as these animals would attack people. I was also very watchful and careful with every step I made as I was barefoot and I did not want to step on broken glass and, especially, a poisonous snake.

During those days, Mr. Manson, the white overseer, drank water first from the jug. I watched as he drank water and released dark-brown chewing-tobacco saliva into the jug. The once-clear drinking water now had a brown tint. Because of extremely hot weather, some fieldworkers drank the brown water, while others refused. They waited until lunchtime and walked a mile to the manual pump to get clean drinking water to put in their personal mason jars. I always drank clean, fresh water at the pump.

Grandfather Little eventually cut a garden hoe's handle in half to accommodate my height. I used the hoe to chop tall grass from the cotton on the mile-long cotton rows. Chopping the grass away from the cotton stalks allowed the cotton to expand and grow faster. Grass robbed nutrients and fertilizer in the soil from cotton. Oftentimes, the hot sand in the cotton field burned my bare feet.

My pay remained the same for chopping cotton, $2 a day (ten-hour workdays). Every two weeks, when I got paid, my grandfather charged me $1 for room and board. His life lesson to me was "You always pay room and board when you live in another person's house. Nothing is free."

MY PAYCHECK SHORTAGE

When I received my second paycheck, I noticed it was short $6, or three days' pay. I mentioned this to my grandfather, and he said, "Let it go, because this happens to cotton fieldworkers all the time." They were afraid to approach the white overseer regarding pay shortages.

I know fear existed in the black community in Mount Gilead. This stemmed from the murder of a young black male named Harry. Harry was one of my childhood friends. It was alleged that white males saw Harry walking down a country road. They abducted him, used rope to tie him to their car's bumper, and dragged him for miles until he died. They left Harry's dead body lying in a ditch. This incident created a lot of fear and resentment.

I disobeyed my grandfather and approached Mr. Manson and told him my paycheck had a pay shortage of $6. His face turned red as a traffic stop sign as he gave me an angry look. He then tried to stare me down, but I stared right back at him. Fieldworkers stopped chopping cotton to listen to our conversation. After a while, the overseer felt embarrassed with the fieldworkers staring at him. He finally conceded and said, "Kenneth, I will bring you a new paycheck on Monday." As promised, that Monday, he gave me the correct dollar amount on my paycheck.

That night after work, I overheard my grandfather telling my grandmother that I went to Mr. Manson about my paycheck shortage after he told me not to do it. He laughed and said, "That is one stubborn boy!" Their conversation ended in loud laughter about Mr. Manson's face turning red when "that boy" approached him.

During that summer, other young fieldworkers approached Mr. Manson regarding their pay shortages too. He eventually paid the young fieldworkers.

I also worked other summer jobs, such as harvesting cucumbers, cantaloupes, peaches, watermelons, and tobacco. Sometimes I was paid $5 per day (ten-hour days) to harvest produce. Black fieldworkers used mules to transport tobacco from the field to a large insulated tobacco barn. They hung the tobacco in a large barn to dry out, and it was later sold by the same family member to tobacco buyers.

I had other nonpaying jobs with my grandfather, such as feeding pigs and chickens, making structural repairs to the pigpen and chicken coup, and cutting firewood for cooking. My grandmother also had me working in her vegetable garden. I also picked blackberries for my grandmother to can in mason jars.

PICKING BLACKBERRIES AND RED BUGS

The downside of picking blackberries was, my body became infested with little insects called red bugs. They migrated to my body's private area (scrotum) and dug in under my skin. I repeatedly scratched the itchy bumps.

Grandmother Little used a safety pin to dig out red bugs and applied rubbing alcohol to my private area, and that always created a strong, burning sensation. I would run outside, drop my short pants and underwear, and sat in a foot tub of cold water to eliminate the burning sensation.

MY FIRST LEARNING EXPERIENCE WITH A MULE

Grandfather Little also taught me how to guide a mule to plow farmland. The old gray mule, named Bette, belonged to Mr. Little, a white descendant of the former plantation owner. Bette lived in a barn right behind Mr. Little's big white house. My grandfather taught me commands for guiding Bette, such as "Giddy up" to move forward, "Gee" to move left, "Ha" to move right, and "Whoa" to stop the mule. One day, my grandfather drove his car home from the big white house and allowed me to ride Bette home alone. I was so excited!

My grandparents' house was approximately two miles through the woods from the big white house. Just for fun, I decided to see just how fast Bette could run. She galloped about ten yards and came to a complete stop. I kept saying, "Giddy up, Bette!" but she would not move. I gently rubbed her neck and quietly asked her to move. About thirty minutes later, she started walking very slowly. This experience gave credence to the expression "Stubborn as a mule."

Bette made me think about myself, as Grandfather Little and other family members always called me stubborn. My grandparents and family members called me stubborn when I shared my lofty dreams and visions of a better life. They could not convince me to scale back on my dreams and visions. In common terms, I had the big head. I proudly wore these labels from childhood to adulthood. I viewed labels as a compliment as no one, including my parents, could deter me from my visions and dreams of being successful. Yes, call me stubborn or big head—the label fits!

My grandfather was standing in the yard when I arrived. He wanted to know what took me so long. Before I could come up with a good lie, he advised me that a mule does not run fast like a horse. "You have been watching too many cowboy shows on television." He then told me to climb down and hook Bette up to the plow and start plowing in the cornfield.

I spent my summers with my grandparents doing manual labor. This was my grandfather's loving way of grooming me to become a hardworking, responsible man like my father. My grandfather's life lesson to me was "A child's idle mind is the devil's workshop." He also said, "If you are working, you cannot get into devilment [trouble]." My grandfather allowed me to have Sundays off work. This was a day when I could play and relax.

GRANDMOTHER LITTLE WORKING AT THE BIG WHITE HOUSE

On selected days, Grandmother Little worked at the big white house. She cooked for and cleaned the house of the former slave owner's descendant, Mr. Little. She did not get paid for doing the work. Since my grandparents lived free on his land and in one of his run-down, substandard old houses, he thought my grandmother's work at the big house was fair compensation. I strongly disagreed with this concept. However, my father was born in that old house.

Late one evening, I observed Mr. Little driving my grandmother home in his big black Buick. My grandmother always rode home sitting in the back seat of the car. One evening, I asked her, "Why do you ride in the back instead of the front seat?" She replied. "I have to maintain my dignity as a married woman, and I do not want people saying that I am involved with that man." I started quietly thinking to myself that since Mr. Little's white father was my grandmother's father, he was really my grandmother's white brother. I was afraid to say this out loud to my grandmother. There were some black women who rode in the front seat of Mr. Little's car. Neighbors did spread vicious rumors about them.

END OF SUMMER

At the end of each summer, my mother would take most of the money I saved to buy herself more stylish clothes and shoes. She spent limited money on my school clothes and shoes. This really made me angry.

CHAPTER 16

FAMILY MOVED FROM BADIN TO NEW HOUSE IN NEW LONDON, NORTH CAROLINA

During my third-grade school year in 1957, my parents built a new house in a rural area. Before building the house, we had to use axes and chain saws to cut down large oak and pine trees and vines on approximately two acres of land. Eventually, my father hired a bull-dozer operator to level off a portion of the land to build the house. The house was beautiful after it was built. The house's exterior had white Sheetrock and redbrick. The interior had hardwood floors in the hallway, living room, and three bedrooms. The house also had a large kitchen, an indoor bathroom, and a one-car garage. The remaining of the cleared property was for vegetable garden space and a remote area for raising pigs and chickens.

The new house was three miles from Badin. My mailing address was now listed under New London, North Carolina.

Because of segregation, I was still required to ride the school bus for three miles to attend West Badin School.

It was a relief for me to move from Badin to rural New London. We had moved into four different houses in Badin in two years because my mother was not friendly toward our neighbors. When my mother drank alcohol, she would start arguments with neighbors or flirt with men in the neighborhood. Further, when she was intoxicated, I would hide because I did not want to trigger any of her physical or verbal abuse toward me. When she was intoxicated, her behavior made me mentally revert to age five in Mount Gilead, North Carolina. That day, I was so afraid walking through the woods as she held my hand, cursing and accusing me of causing her to have a nervous breakdown. That was a dark day in my young life.

Moving to the rural area brought on new challenges for me. I got out of bed early each morning and walked a mile through the woods to catch the school bus. I felt a lot of anxiety walking through the woods. I anticipated that something bad was going to happen to me in those woods. My stomach was nervous, and beads of sweat formed on my forehead and face.

One day, I told my mother I was afraid of walking through the woods to catch the bus. The old red dirt road was heavily surrounded by numerous tall oak and pine trees. Residents did hunt for wild game in these woods. Just to keep peace, I did not mention how walking through the woods triggered my anxiety.

Eventually, my mother telephoned the school principal, Mr. Black, and told him that I should not have to walk a mile through the woods to catch the school bus. She added that she feared for my safety, as walking alone through the woods in early morning and late afternoon was dangerous. After a lengthy argument, Mr. Black agreed to stop requiring me to walk through the woods. I then walked half a mile from our house on a highway to catch the bus.

On the first day of my new bus route, the bus driver harassed me. He said his bus route changed and it was my fault. He added that he must get out of bed earlier to drive students to school. I was very embarrassed as students on the bus laughed at me.

That afternoon, when I arrived home from school, I told my mother about the bus driver's behavior. The next afternoon, my mother was waiting at the bus stop and cursed at the bus driver for harassing me. Students laughed out of control at the bus driver. He was so embarrassed and never harassed me again.

In my mind, regarding these school situations, my mother made me feel like she cared for me.

MY FATHER CATCHES MY MOTHER OUT ON A DATE WITH MR. PIMP

After a short time of us living in the new house in New London, another explosive situation occurred. Since our new house was in a rural, wooded area, my mother regularly walked through the woods to meet her lover, Mr. Pimp. He drove below the house and picked her up. My mother did not know she was being watched by Mr. Hope, our white neighbor. He lived roughly one hundred yards through the woods from our new house. He was always in the woods, making illegal moonshine liquor to sell.

One day, while my mother was away, Mr. Hope saw my father in the woods feeding his thirty pigs. He told my father that my mother walked through the woods near his house to meet a man. He described the color, make, and model of the man's truck. He also told my father to drive home on the back road to catch them. After getting off work one afternoon, my father decided to drive home using the back road instead of the main highway. Mr. Hope's spying on my mother paid off. My father caught my mother and Mr. Pimp riding together, hugging and kissing on the back road. My father was livid when I came home from school.

I asked my father, "Why are you so angry?" He replied, "I just caught your mother out on a date with Mr. Pimp." He went on to say, "I used Mr. Hope's information to catch your mother riding in Mr. Pimp's pickup truck, hugging and kissing." My father said my mother's eyes got big when she glanced through the truck's rear window and saw him following them.

He said, "I considered running them off the road into a steep ditch, but at the last minute, I decided they were not worth it. I drove around them, waved, and came on home." My mother stayed at a girlfriend's house for a few days to avoid my father.

A few days later, a classmate approached me at school and asked me to deliver a message from my mother to my father. She said, "Your mother wants you to ask your father if she could come home." I relayed the message to him. He pondered it for a while, and to my surprise, he told me, "Get on your bicycle and go to your mother's girlfriend's house and tell her to come home."

I begged my father not to beat her, and he promised not to touch her. And he kept his word. My father's light-skinned complexion turned red when my mother walked into the house.

My classmate laughed and told other students about my mother getting caught on a date with Mr. Pimp. They teased me about my mother and her behavior. Although it was wrong, I said to them, "You cannot talk about my mother! You need to look at your unfaithful parents!"

CHAPTER 17

DISCOVERED MY TALL TREE WITH LARGE GREEN LEAVES

At the age of eight, in early spring, feeling down and depressed about my life, I discovered a tall tree near our new house. The tall tree had lots of large green leaves, and it appeared to be the perfect hiding place for me. I climbed high into the tall tree, talked to the green leaves, and told them my name was Kenneth. The tree leaves became my alter ego or trusted "companions" and welcomed me.

The tall tree was my refuge from my turbulent life. I often shared my life's stories and philosophies with the green tree leaves. For example, I compared my life with a salmon's. I told the green tree leaves that during mating season, salmon swim upstream against strong river currents to lay eggs—their eggs spawn new life. I go through life facing strong currents of abuse, and my life's struggles spawn hardship and pain. The tree leaves "told me" to stay in faith as life would not be like this always. My day would come.

MR. HOPE'S ILLEGAL MOONSHINE LIQUOR STILL

One afternoon after school, my father was waiting at home for me. He asked me, "Did you tamper with Mr. Hope's liquor still (large cooper kettles used to make illegal moonshine liquor) in the woods?" I confessed that when my friends and I were looking for berries to pick, we saw the liquor still and moved in closer to examine it. As we approached the still, we broke the thin black sewing thread that was tied to trees around the still's perimeter. Broken thread lets a bootlegger know that someone or police officers had located the still.

I told my father that after we discovered the still, we soon walked away and did not damage it. I believed Mr. Hope must have been hiding in the woods and recognized us. My father then told me, "Stay away from the still." It was obvious to me that Mr. Hope and my father had become close friends.

FOURTH GRADE, 1958

Later that spring, I was happy to be promoted to the fourth grade. Looking ahead, I knew I had a tough challenge because Mrs. Battle was my new teacher. She had a reputation of being the toughest but best teacher at West Badin. Mrs. Battle was a dark-skinned lady with mixed gray hair and stood around five feet five inches tall. She had a beautiful smile, was well-dressed in fashionable suits each day, and displayed an air of confidence when she walked and talked.

She was a strict disciplinarian. When students disobeyed her, she made them bend over to get lashes with a yardstick. Mrs. Battle taught at West Badin for several decades. She taught most of my classmates' parents and grandparents. Because Mrs. Battle was so tough, she earned the nickname Bob Steele (a tough cowboy on television at that time). Being fearful of Mrs. Battle, I asked my mother if I could transfer to another fourth-grade teacher's class. She answered no without explanation.

One day, Mrs. Battle spoke with me about being shy and having low self-esteem. She asked me, "Why do you always look down when you speak to me?" I told her, "I don't think I am as good as you." She then asked, "Why do you think that way?" I said, "You went to college, wear nice clothes, and people respect you and do not laugh at you." She then told me, "Stand up and make eye contact with me." She put her hands on my shoulders and whispered to me in a commanding voice, "Do not ever let me hear you say that again. God loves you, Kenneth, and so do I!"

Mrs. Battle gave me a big hug in front of the class. I promised to never say those words again. I was on cloud nine and made a promise to myself to never forget Mrs. Battle's words.

Every Monday morning, Mrs. Battle would say a fervent prayer for her students. The students had to learn the Lord's Prayer by heart and repeat it each school day. I started feeling secure after listening to Mrs. Battle's heartfelt prayers and reciting the Lord's Prayer.

It was common knowledge around the Badin community that my quiet personality evolved from constant emotional bashing. In my opinion, my mother suffered from an untreated bipolar condition. To escape the emotional bashing and physical beatings, I often climbed high into the tall tree. I told the large green tree leaves that I wanted to grow up to be a good person like Mrs. Battle.

Like Mrs. Battle, I wanted to show my confidence when I walked and talked. I also wanted to dress like a professional and command respect. I often talked to the green tree leaves about the respect I had for Mrs. Battle. The tree leaves encouraged me to make her my role model. Each time I climbed the tree, I would hide up there for three to four hours a day dreaming about the future.

I noticed that Mrs. Battle would always pay attention to my behavior in class and constantly called on me to answer questions. This forced me to study hard and do my homework assignments every night. Each day for a week, right before Christmas break, Mrs. Battle gave the class final exams. I received an A on my first and all the following exams. I also received an A on my handwriting exam, and Mrs. Battle posted it on the classroom board. I was really elated when I saw my name posted on the "A honor roll!" My self-esteem went through the roof.

CELEBRATING CHRISTMAS WITH THE LITTLE FAMILY

In late December, after school closed, I spent the two-week Christmas break at Grandfather and Grandmother Little's house in Mount Gilead. My father drove down from New London on selected days to go hunting for wild game with his friends. They would return late afternoon and drink illegal moonshine.

Grandfather Little would sneak into the kitchen and have a few drinks of his homemade fermented wild cherry wine. One day, I secretly sampled a taste of his wine. It had a sweet, smooth taste. Even though the wine had a good taste, it made me feel light-headed.

As a tradition, Grandfather Little and I would go into the woods to cut down a fresh Christmas tree. The fresh tree provided a beautiful evergreen fragrance in the cold, drafty old house.

Grandmother Little and Aunt Ellen were responsible for decorating the tree. They shucked homegrown popcorn off corncobs and popped it in homemade butter on the wood-burning stove. After it cooled, they gave me a needle and white thread to make long strings of white garland to wrap around the tree. We drew, colored with crayon, and cut out paper pictures of Santa Claus, reindeer, elves, and other Christmas characters to hang on the tree. We used cardboard to draw and cut out the image of a star. The star was wrapped in aluminum foil and placed on the top of the tree. To imitate snow, we used self-rising flour to dust the tree. Large multicolored Christmas light bulbs made the tree come alive.

Christmas day was always a fun-loving day at my grandparents' house. Even though they did not have a lot of money to buy expensive gifts, I felt love flow throughout that cold, drafty old house. The house was full of family and friends' loud laughter celebrating Christmas. Each year, my grandparents gave me a pair of socks or a box of chocolate-covered cherries as a Christmas gift. These small but precious gifts made me so happy. It was my grandparents' love and kindness that mattered most to me.

EATING GRANDMOTHER LITTLE'S AND AUNT ELLEN'S CHRISTMAS TREATS

The kitchen table was full of delicious homemade holiday desserts. These desserts included peanut butter cake, coconut cake, chocolate cake, fruitcake, plain yellow cake, banana pudding, sweet potato pies, and others.

I was in and out of the kitchen all day long, sampling various desserts. Neighbors from near and far stopped by the house to eat desserts.

Family members, neighbors, and I ate a lot of the delicious desserts. Before leaving my grandparents' house, everyone had to make a comfort stop at the smelly old wooden outdoor toilet. This caused a shortage of old newspapers and magazines that lined the toilet floor. These items were used as toilet paper during those days.

RETURNING TO FOURTH GRADE AFTER CHRISTMAS BREAK

When I returned to school after Christmas break, I did not break my stride. I continued to make the "A honor roll."

During that spring, my father was laid off from his job with Alcoa as he did not have enough seniority to keep his job. This was a result of him staying in New York too long after being discharged from the US Army after World War II. Our family's quality of life declined sharply. He could no longer afford twenty-five cents per day for me to eat a hot lunch in the school cafeteria.

One morning, Mrs. Battle asked, "Kenneth, where is your lunch money?" I explained, "My father was laid off at Alcoa, so I have to bring my lunch from home." She had a painful look on her face after I told her my father was laid off from Alcoa.

Early on school mornings, my mother or father would get out of bed to deep-fry rabbit or squirrel. This was wild game my father brought home from hunting trips. The deep-fried meat was placed on two slices of white bread for my lunch. I brought this sandwich to school wrapped in wax paper and placed in a brown paper bag. By lunchtime, my brown bag lunch was soaked with meat grease from deep-frying. Students who brought their lunch to school had to remain at their desk to eat their lunch while other students went to the school cafeteria to eat a hot lunch.

Sometimes I placed my greasy sandwich in the back pocket of my blue jeans and asked Mrs. Battle for permission to use the restroom. I hid in the restroom long enough to eat my greasy sandwich. The greasy sandwich saturated my blue jeans' back pocket and underwear. I just wanted to avoid being teased by my classmates about my greasy brown bag lunch. I especially did not want them to know that I brought fried rabbit or squirrel for lunch. Some days I threw my lunch in the trash can to avoid teasing. On these afternoons, I ate like a horse at dinnertime at home.

Eventually, my father found a job doing janitorial work at a local cotton mill. His weekly salary was less than half the money he earned working for Alcoa, but still, this job helped to slightly improve our quality of life.

Later that spring, I was happy to be promoted to the fifth grade, but I did not want to leave Mrs. Battle. I loved her very much as she gave my self-esteem a huge boost.

MY FATHER'S HOMEMADE SYRUP

One morning, my father taught me a life lesson on how to improvise while cooking breakfast. He added flour and water into a bowl and hand-stirred it until it became thick pancake batter. He cooked the pancake batter in a black cast-iron frying pan filled with hot pork lard grease (shortening).

After cooking the pancakes, he noticed we did not have syrup. I was disappointed as I really wanted pancakes, syrup, and fried pork fatback meat for breakfast. He paused for a second and said, "Watch this, boy!" He then added water to the large black iron frying pan. When the water came to a boil, he slowly stirred granulated white sugar into the pan. The sugar melted and thickened and became substitute syrup for my pancakes. My father really made me happy that morning—my breakfast was delicious!

MY SERIOUS ILLNESS

During my fifth-grade year, I became very ill. For several days, I had excruciating pain in the lower right side of my stomach. At first, my parents thought I was constipated and gave me a laxative to clean my system. However, the pain continued. They finally decided to take me to Dr. Rankin's office in Badin. After examining me, he quickly concluded that I had appendicitis. Dr. Rankin told my parents to put me in the car and rush me to Stanly County Hospital's emergency room in Albemarle, North Carolina. The hospital was located seven miles from Badin.

Dr. Rankin immediately telephoned the hospital staff and told them to prepare to perform emergency appendix-removal surgery on a nine-year-old colored boy. He also told them that my parents were driving me to the hospital. My appendix had burst, and it was life-threatening. Dr. Roxy of the hospital staff performed the emergency appendix surgery. After the successful surgery, I was placed in a bed located in the hospital hallway. During that era, the hospital was segregated, and white patients had priority of being placed in hospital rooms. After a few white patients were discharged, I was eventually placed in a hospital room for two weeks with another black male, named Mr. Roberts. It was hard for me to understand why patients had to be separated.

Although my surgery was successful, Dr. Roxy later told my parents that if they had waited one more day, the poison from my ruptured appendix would have killed me. This was a tender moment as my parents showed great concern for me. After I had recovered two months after, Dr. Rankin, my primary care doctor, released me to return to school. I am grateful to God for continuing to hold me in His loving arms, embracing and protecting me.

FIFTH GRADE, 1959

Mrs. Nelson was my fifth-grade teacher. Like Mrs. Battle, she had a beautiful smile, was well dressed in fashionable suits each day, and displayed an air of confidence when she walked and talked.

Mrs. Nelson showed great patience and compassion toward me when I returned to school after my illness. She monitored my school recess activities while I played with my classmates. She would not allow me to wrestle with the boys for fear of injuring my appendix surgery area.

Mrs. Nelson also tutored me, one-on-one, on schoolwork I missed while absent from school. She quickly brought me up to speed with my classmates. I made decent grades on my report card—As, Bs, and Cs. Later that spring, I was promoted to the sixth grade. During this time, I really loved Mrs. Battle and Mrs. Nelson as they both showed compassion toward me.

CHAPTER 18

ESCAPE FROM REALITY

One very windy day, I climbed high into my favorite tall tree. I was fearful and clung tightly to the wavering tree branches as the turbulent wind blew. I shouted out to the green tree leaves, "I wish I had a rope to tightly tie my body to you to prevent the wind from tossing me back and forth!" The green tree leaves told me to calm down and stretch out on my inner faith as God was still watching over me. Immediately, there was calm, and my fear disappeared.

This experience triggered memories of my younger life. Looking back, I was age five again, reliving horrific experiences I had at the hands of my mother. Was this a sign that I had early stages of post-traumatic stress disorder (PTSD)? Each time in my life, when my fear elevated, I would mentally return to that dark episode with my mother. It appeared that this episode was deeply etched and frozen in my memory. I concluded in my young mind that something was mentally wrong with Mother as I was often the target of her frustration. I also wondered if I would grow up and inherit my mother's abusive behavior. I did not want to continue this mean, abusive behavioral cycle as an adult with my children.

I tried hard to make my mother love me as much as I loved

her. At the age of five, I walked a great distance to the local hand-operated pump to get buckets of water for the house and worked with her to clean Mrs. Daisy's big white house. My mother was angry about cleaning to earn a small amount of pocket change.

At home, she boasted about how she survived alone in New York City, danced on glass floors in upscale nightclubs in Harlem, and wore the finest clothes and shoes. She angrily expressed, "Cleaning a white woman's house is beneath me!" Again, I was the target of her frustrations. I continued trying to reach out to her to show my love, but the abuse continued.

When I did a fast-forward from the age of five to the present, I dreaded the inevitable—I had to climb down from the tall tree and go into the house. My stomach was nervous, and my hands were sweaty. I tried to maintain a low profile as I quietly entered the house. I so badly wished my family house would turn into a loving home.

GREEN TREE LEAVES IN WINTER HIBERNATION

I became deeply depressed during fall and winter months as my friends, the green tree leaves, would change colors and fade away. I felt exposed and lonely in the naked tall tree. I was afraid of climbing high up in the tall tree during these months as hunters were in the woods, searching for wild game. I did not want to be mistaken for wild game such as squirrels, raccoons, or birds nestled in the tall tree. I longed for the spring season to return. I waited for my green tree leaves to bloom again.

WELCOME BACK, GREEN TREE LEAVES

During the spring, after the green tree leaves bloomed, I was happy and climbed the tall tree to welcome them back. We talked about their hibernation during the fall and winter and discussed how much we missed one another. I told them that Mrs. Battle and Skip's loving spirit watched over me during their absence. Each day, I felt Skip's loving presence.

The green tree leaves served as my fortress of protection and helped me maintain my mental well-being. I often confided in them regarding hurt and pain I suffered in the house. I imagined, each time the cool wind blew, the swaying green leaves embracing and showing me their love and affection. This had to be God's way of giving me comfort and protecting me from hurt, harm, and danger. For this, I say thank You, God, from the bottom of my heart! It is a true saying that God will not allow harm to come to those who love Him. Looking back, little did I know that God was laying a solid foundation to build a young boy who grew into a mentally strong, resilient, responsible man. God never allowed abuse to conquer me.

One day, an airplane flew high above my tall tree and I dreamed that one day I would fly on an airplane in search of fulfilling my dreams and visions. In addition to dreaming in the tall tree during the day, I had fascinating dreams at night. At night, I envisioned the day when I could venture out of my present environment to look for love, travel the world, join the military, get a college degree, get a great-paying white-collar job, get married, buy a house, have a loving family, and fulfill my visions and dreams. I would never let go of my dreams, my visions, and the wonderful thoughts of my green tree leaves, Mrs. Battle, and Skip.

CHAPTER 19

ANOTHER SUMMER WITH GRANDFATHER AND GRANDMOTHER LITTLE

That summer, I returned to my grandparents' house in Mount Gilead. I chopped cotton and picked peaches, cucumbers, and tobacco. I also plowed the mule and worked in my grandmother's prize-winning vegetable garden. She was so proud of winning first prize in the community competition for the most beautiful vegetable garden. The farm work was hard, but I enjoyed the peace and solitude of living in my grandparents' home during the summer. Their love and kindness embraced me. Their love was a temporary bridge over the troubled waters I experienced at home

SHOPPING IN WADESBORO, NORTH CAROLINA

On selected Saturdays, after getting paid for working in the cotton field, Grandfather Little drove his green Dodge to take the family shopping in Wadesboro, North Carolina. Compared to Mount Gilead, it was a big country town located roughly thirty miles from Mount Gilead. After performing hard, manual labor all week, I always celebrated my accomplishment. I treated myself to two delicious hot dogs loaded with mustard, red-colored coleslaw, beef chili and a soft drink. This was my Saturday treat.

SEVENTH GRADE, 1961

My seventh-grade teacher's name was Mrs. Flythe. She was a stern but gifted academic and music teacher and a talented musician. She made beautiful music playing the piano. This class had a unique arrangement as seventh and eighth grade students shared the same classroom. This was the year I tried to be more positive about my circumstances at home. I tried to change my mind-set and abandon my "woe is me" attitude.

I started to notice my female classmates' physical changes to their bodies. They stopped braiding their hair into pigtails and started using Dixie Peach hair grease and a hot straightening comb to style their hair. They also started to dress in stylish clothes. Sometimes they wore sweet-smelling perfume. My male hormones were raging!

LEARNING TO FRENCH-KISS

One day, while Mrs. Flythe was out of the classroom, an eighth-grade girl asked me if I knew how to French-kiss. I did not have a clue about French-kissing but was willing to fake it. I said yes. She said, "Okay, kiss me!" I quickly gave her a dry kiss on the lips. The girls in the classroom laughed and made fun of me. Fortunately for me, the girl gave me another chance and said, "Let me show you how to French-kiss." She pulled me close and started to slowly move her tongue over my lips and in and out of my mouth. I quickly responded, copying her kissing technique. She then backed away from me, laughed, and walked away.

Her sweet, wet kiss made my hormones explode like fireworks at a Fourth of July celebration. I deliberately allowed traces of her red lipstick to stay on my lips to make my male classmates jealous. That was really a beautiful experience for me. Being young and immature, I fell in love that day!

MY HORMONAL CHANGES

I started to notice my male hormonal changes when I needed stronger masculine deodorant for my flaming underarms. As part of my new nightly routine, I used spray starch to iron my shirt and pants and wash my hair and pack it with stiff hair grease to make waves in my hair. I cut off one of my mother's used silk stockings and placed it on my head to hold my wavy hair in place. To really get the girls' attention, some mornings I secretly splashed on my father's aftershave lotion.

During the fall and winter of my seventh-grade year, my parents made me wear thick cotton long-handle underwear and heavy-duty brogan shoes. In the spring, I did not feel cool as my parents made me wear cheap tennis shoes to school. They refused to buy me a pair of converse tennis shoes. This did not support my wannabe-cool image.

MY BREAKING POINT

Early one Monday morning, a male classmate named Joseph came into the classroom and sat down at his desk directly behind me. He started talking loud about seeing my mother with Mr. Pimp over the weekend. On this day, Joseph's statement about my mother was my breaking point. I was always angry about my mother's ongoing affair with Mr. Pimp.

Sitting at my desk, I started breathing heavily, and suddenly, I jumped up and started giving him fast and furious punches to his face and head. I knocked him out of his chair and down onto the floor. My rage was out of control, and I continued to beat him. My actions convinced me that I could have knocked out the former heavyweight boxing champion of the world Joe Lewis if he had said something bad about my mother.

While I was beating Joseph, I could hear some of my female classmates crying and saying, "Please stop, Kenneth, from beating him!" Some of the boys were saying, "Beat his ass, Kenneth! He shouldn't talk about your mother." Suddenly, Mrs. Flythe entered the classroom and immediately pulled me off him. She escorted both of us to the principal's office. Mr. Black said, "Kenneth, I am surprised to see you in my office. You have never had a behavior problem before! What happened?" I told him, "Joseph was talking loud and saying bad things about my mother." Mr. Black hit me ten times in the palm of my hand with his black leather belt and sent me back to class. I refused to cry from the beating. He also beat Joseph with the leather belt and made him spend the rest of the day on detention in his office. When I returned to the classroom, Mrs. Flythe and my class-mates were quiet and briefly stared at me. I felt so embarrassed about fighting Joseph.

Although my mother was abusive toward me, I still loved my mother. I had reached a point in my life where I did not tolerate negative criticism about my mother from anyone.

PICKING COTTON

During the middle of my seventh-grade year, my father was laid off again from his job with Alcoa. As usual, aluminum sales were slow, and my father did not have enough seniority to keep his job. Again, the quality of life in our house sharply decreased. I eventually had to miss days out of school as we drove to Mount Gilead to pick cotton for limited money. My father told me, "You have to pick one hundred pounds of cotton each day to make some money." Each day, I picked one hundred pounds of cotton as my father requested. It was backbreaking work dragging one hundred pounds of cotton in a large yellow sack. My father and my mother each picked over three hundred pounds of cotton each day. They mastered their cotton-picking skills while growing up on farms in Mount Gilead. My mother often stated, "As a child, your grandfather used dried cotton stalks to beat me if I did not pick three hundred pounds of cotton each day."

In late fall, after the cotton-picking season was over, my mother claimed she developed arthritis from picking cotton. She never consulted with a doctor to get a professional opinion regarding her medical condition. She did; however, put herself on indefinite bed rest. My mother relied on witchcraft to treat her so-called condition. Sometimes the house had a rancid odor from witchcraft medicine.

While in high school, I learned that my mother was involved in witchcraft. One evening, I eavesdropped on her telephone conversation with a so-called preacher and his wife. They advised her that they went to a "root worker" in South Carolina to purchase witchcraft services to put an evil spell on his sister. This was done because his sister refused to give him more money.

I never did find out what happened to the preacher's sister. I did find out later; however, that my mother drove them from North Carolina to South Carolina to see the root worker. After that trip, I could smell rancid odors coming from her dark bedroom. This situation confirmed my suspicion that my mother was involved in witchcraft. I became even more afraid of her as there was no limit to her meanness.

During that time. I knew my life was devoted to Christ and not evil. To me, witchcraft is despicable. I rebuke evil and evildoers in the name of Jesus.

For years, my mother badgered my father, saying, "It is your fault that I developed arthritis and I am now on permanent bed rest." She did; however, get out of bed on selected days to date Mr. Pimp. I firmly believe that, in part, my mother had a bruised ego from picking cotton. Imagine a diva picking cotton!

Because of hard times, my family went to the Salvation Army store to buy used clothes and shoes. It was embarrassing when I went to school one day wearing shoes with shoe soles tied together with clothes hanger wire. This was done to keep the shoe soles from flapping up and down when I walked. My classmates had a field day laughing at me and my old shoes. This experience gave me a strong dose of humility.

CHAPTER 20

MY NEW JOB: CADDIE AT A LOCAL SEGREGATED GOLF COURSE

At the age of twelve, I learned to caddie at the local segregated golf course. I often carried two golf bags on my shoulders for two white golfers, for 18 holes in all types of weather. The local golf course was in Badin across the railroad tracks from West Badin. The golf club house is where white golfers paid green fees to play golf and where they stored their golf clubs.

Young white male caddies were permitted to sit on the front porch while waiting to caddie, free to openly enter the club house and allowed to play golf on the golf course. Young black males were limited to only caddying for white golfers. While waiting for the white golf club professional (golf pro) to call us to caddie, we were restricted to the back of the golf clubhouse. If black males walked around the front without permission, the golf pro and white golfers would say, "Monkeys, get your black asses around back, where you belong." Remarks coming from racists did not faze me. Thanks to my mother's numerous episodes of verbal abuse, I was developing thick skin.

Black males also worked as greens-keepers on the golf course. They performed manual labor, such as mowing golf greens and fairways, and other backbreaking activities. They were supervised by a white male.

I earned on average $8 to $10 per weekend caddying. My mother gave me $2 of this money weekly to buy lunch at school. She kept the remainder of the money. From the age of twelve to seventeen, I worked as a caddie almost every weekend and on holidays. Because I made more money as a caddie, I no longer spent summers with my loving grandparents in Mount Gilead. I missed being with my grandparents, but I did not miss the hard work in cotton and other fields for less pay.

From a personal perspective, while caddying, I learned the theory and techniques of the game of golf. During that era, golf was called a gentleman's game and governed by a strict honor system. For example, if a golfer hit his golf ball into the woods, to comply with the honor system, he was not allowed to move the ball without adding a stroke to his score on that hole. Most golfers did comply with the honor system.

Later in life, I bought state-of-the-art golf clubs and played almost every weekend, rain or shine. This was a positive outcome for me and other caddies. We learned to caddie on a segregated golf course and eventually refined our skills as golfers.

EIGHTH GRADE, 1962

I was promoted to the eighth grade in the spring. Mr. Devine was my eighth-grade teacher. He had a tall muscular build and wore fashionable suits to school each day. Mr. Devine was also the school's football and basketball coach and, at times, served as acting principal. As mentioned earlier, West Badin School had years of winning football and basketball championships. Mr. Devine was the gifted coach for these teams. He commanded respect and maintained excellent relationships with his high school athletes. A lot of his athletes graduated from high school and went on to become star athletes in colleges.

Mr. Devine was also an excellent classroom teacher. Students paid close attention to his class lectures and excelled academically in his classroom. I continued to make As, Bs, and Cs in his class. I was promoted to the ninth grade in the spring.

NINTH GRADE, 1963

Ninth grade was considered high school at West Badin School. This was the year when high school students reported to their home-room teacher each morning and changed classes throughout the school day. Changing classes was required for all students from the ninth grade through twelfth. Mrs. Goins was my ninth-grade home-room teacher.

Attending elementary and middle schools challenged my poor social and interpersonal skills of interacting with students. I was terrified of being in classes and trying to interact with the high school students, who were older. They seemed to be happy, self-assured, well-dressed, fun-loving, and outgoing.

My self-esteem was again in the toilet. I started making poor grades again in school as I was too bashful to speak out in class. I often wondered what happened to me since the fourth grade. Back then, I excelled academically and had renewed self-esteem that Mrs. Battle developed. I wondered if I was like my mother, suffering from a mental health condition stemming from physical and verbal abuse.

SCHOOL ACTIVITIES AND HOUSE PARTIES

I lacked confidence to fully participate in high school activities and private parties. These parties were in dark rooms at teenagers' houses in West Badin. Teenagers were secretly drinking alcohol, laughing, hugging and kissing, hand dancing, and slow dragging (couples dancing close to each other on slow, romantic love songs).

Attending teenagers' house parties reminded me of being age five again. I was at the bootlegger's house with my parents in Mount Gilead. Back then, I sat on the floor in a dark room and quietly laughed at intoxicated adults trying to dance to loud jukebox music.

But now, as a teenager, I stood in a dark corner of the party room and quietly laughed at intoxicated teenagers dancing to loud music. Living in rural New London did not afford me the opportunity to learn and practice dancing. Further, my mother did not allow me to play music in the house as she said music got on her nerves. She also called it devil's music. I developed a passion for listening to music by visiting other people's homes. I always asked if I could listen to music on their stereo. During that time, a stereo was used to play plastic records or the radio.

I really wanted to break my cycle of poor social and interpersonal skills. But how? I spent most of my time hiding in my tall tree, talking to green tree leaves, or doing manual labor.

Sometimes I felt invisible. I missed being in Mrs. Battle's fourth-grade class. It was obvious to me, five years later, the self-esteem she instilled in me had diminished because of my mother's outrageous, mean behavior. I did, of course, maintain a passion for selected school subjects, such as social studies, history, and English literature. I loved to read and interpret poems.

I continued to caddie at the golf course on weekends and

holidays. There were times when I sneaked away from school during the week to caddie and earn money. Some days, Mr. Black drove by the golf course, looking for students skipping school. At that time, I thought he was just harassing us. As I look back now with a more mature outlook on life, I can see Mr. Black's action demonstrated his commitment to educating black students.

TENTH GRADE, 1964

My insecurities continued in the tenth grade. My school grades and social and interpersonal skills continued to sharply decline. Then one day, I received some good news from my cousin Malerie Richardson that really rocked my world. She told me her girlfriend Malinda Houston had a crush on me and wanted to be my girlfriend. She also shared Malinda's home telephone number with me.

Malinda was short, petite, and very pretty, with a beautiful smile. My first impression was that she was light-years ahead of me in terms of maturity. I was too nervous to call her immediately. I felt like a dog running in circles, chasing his tail. I just did not know what to do.

Eventually, I climbed my tall sycamore tree to consult with the green tree leaves regarding the affairs of my heart. On that day, a cool breeze caused the tree to smoothly rock back and forth. The mood was right for me to talk to the green tree leaves about Malinda Houston. They smiled and were elated to learn that I was ready to get involved with a beautiful young lady. We did a group hug! Most times when we hugged, I imagined the green tree leaves being the size of elephant ears. I felt secure when they warmly embraced me.

They touted that a young lady loved a well-dressed young man. They immediately advised me to upgrade my wardrobe. Go to a men's department store in Albemarle, North Carolina, and have a layaway (will call) on fashionable clothes to impress her.

One day, while caddying, I asked the white golfer, "What is the name of the expensive cologne you are wearing?" I also asked, "Where did you buy it?" I went on to tell him that I was trying to impress a young lady.

He laughed and said, "It is English Leather, and I could buy it at a men's store in Albemarle, North Carolina."

I later caught a ride to the men's store, purchased some clothes on layaway, and put the cologne on a payment plan as well.

The green tree leaves also advised me to telephone Malinda at home and engage her in a general conversation that focused mostly on her. They instructed me to tell Malinda that I admired her academic skills and athletic ability on the girl's high school basketball team.

I waited a few days and made a telephone call to Malinda's house one evening after school. Her mother answered the telephone and I got choked up and could barely say a word. I finally said, "Good afternoon, Mrs. Houston, my name is Kenneth Little. May I speak to Malinda, please?"

She kindly said, "Hold on," and called Malinda to the telephone. I was very nervous on the telephone call and was at a loss for words. Fortunately, Malinda chimed in and did most of the talking.

Having a girlfriend was a new frontier for me to explore. We talked to each other at school every day and every night on the telephone. I fell deeply in love with Malinda. Her favorite treats were barbecue potato chips and pinto beans. Our favorite song was by Curtis Mayfield featuring the Impressions, titled "I'm So Proud." The lyrics to this song became deeply entrenched in my heart.

Trouble soon erupted. My mother noticed I was happy, dressing better, wearing expensive cologne, and talking on the telephone every night. She cursed at me and told me, "Stop interacting with Malinda!" She went on to say, "High school girls' only motive is to get pregnant." My mother then said, "I am not going to pay for a baby!"

A thought quickly entered my mind. How could my mother pay for anything? After all, she did not have a job. At that stage of my life, I had not entertained the thought of having sex. Or did I?

It was amazing to me that my mother married my father when she was in the tenth grade. The Little family accused her of being a gold digger, because my father had a good-paying job working for Alcoa Aluminum Company in Badin, North Carolina. They also accused her of running away from her dysfunctional family. I had no intention of getting married in the tenth grade.

I was quiet, but inside I was furious with my mother for making mean statements, especially considering her tarnished reputation and extramarital affairs. I was defiant and disobeyed my mother. I did not immediately break off my relationship with Malinda. Again, I was deeply in love with her. I regret that I never openly talked to Malinda about my mother's behavior. I was afraid.

INCIDENT AT STANLY COUNTY FAIR

Each September, the Stanly County Fair was sponsored in Albemarle, North Carolina. On student day, all school students received free tickets at school to attend the fair. School closed around noon on that day to allow students to go home and go to the fair. My mother drove me to the fair and gave me a time to meet her outside the fair gate to go home. I went inside and had a beautiful, romantic evening with Malinda.

I waited outside the fair gate at the designated time to meet my mother. She showed up late from her date with Mr. Pimp. I knew she had been with Mr. Pimp, because a classmate told me that he saw them together. She parked the car and decided to make a horrific scene in front of hundreds of people at the fair.

She approached me and started cursing, slapping, and scratching me in the face, accusing me of not coming out on time. I did not flinch while she was abusing me; I just stared at her. Eventually, she grew tired after repeatedly scratching and hitting me. Although I was hurting inside from humiliation, I smiled and walked toward the car. This really made her furious.

On the way home, she cursed and said, "I will kill you if you don't leave Malinda alone!" When we arrived at the house, she told my father, "It is that hardheaded fool's fault that we arrived home late." She was really trying to cast the stink off her trail as she was late getting back from her date with Mr. Pimp. I was livid but was smart enough to keep quiet.

The next school day, students laughed and harassed me about my embarrassing public beating from my mother. I dismissed their negative comments. By the age of fifteen, I had developed thick skin regarding students' and adults' negative comments about my mother. From the ages five to fifteen, it was repeatedly the same old town gossip about my mother. At that time, I went on the offensive; when people approached me with negative comments about my mother, I fired back with insults about their families. That made most people slow their roll.

MY FORCED BREAKUP WITH MALINDA

The next night, my mother stood beside me on the telephone with a stick in her hand and forced me to tell Malinda we had to break off our relationship. I was devastated as I loved Malinda so much. I was really angry with my mother and her double standards. I harbored resentment toward my mother for years. Malinda and I were victims of my mother's mean behavior and untreated mental health condition. My father kept a low profile during this situation.

I think he was glad that my mother left him alone and directed her anger at me.

My mother's mean behavior continued toward me and my future girlfriends. The major premise for her behavior was twofold: she figured (1) I would withhold money from her and spend it on my girlfriends and (2) to keep me isolated in rural New London and prevent me from crossing paths with her while she committed adultery in Badin and elsewhere. Her primary focus—and she constantly reminded me of this—was that she could take every dollar I earned until I reached the age of twenty-one. The money I earned was used to support her lavish taste for expensive clothes and shoes.

I became familiar with the term indentured servant in my tenth-grade history class. According to Webster's Dictionary, an indentured servant is a person who is bound and must work for another person for a specified time to gain freedom. I felt like an indentured servant to my mother. That spring, I was promoted to the eleventh grade.

TALKING TO GREEN TREE LEAVES

CHAPTER 21

SUMMER VACATION WITH MY GRANDPARENTS IN NEWPORT NEWS, VIRGINIA

A surprise move after school closed for the summer—my mother sent me by bus to Newport News, Virginia, to visit Grandfather and Grandmother Gould. This was really a move to get me away from Malinda. Rather than being angry, I looked forward to being away from the abuse.

Grandmother Gould always gave me money to ride the city bus to visit Uncle Jacob, Aunt Laney, and my cousins in Hampton, Virginia. I had fun going to movies and to the beach and hanging out with their friends. They joked with me about my North Carolina accent. They did not offend me by calling me a country boy too.

One evening, Grandmother Gould and I sat on the front porch, laughing and talking. Grandfather Gould told Grandmother Gould he was going to visit his preacher buddies. After he drove away, my grandmother laughed and said, "Your grandfather really put on his suit and tie and cologne to go visit his girlfriend on

Sixteenth Street in Newport News." She then laughed and added, "I am not thinking about that crazy man, just as long as he continues to pay the bills." I laughed out loud too.

NEW LOVER

Suddenly, from two houses down the block, a young lady named Mandy stopped by to visit my grandmother. My grandmother introduced us, got up, and went inside the house. She was really sitting in the living room with the window up, listening to our conversation. Mandy told me, "I am entering my sophomore year in high school, and I am an honor student." She was a year younger than me. I told her, "I am entering my junior year in high school, and I was an honor student once upon a time." We both laughed.

My eyes slowly surveyed her body and nice clothes as I inhaled the sweet fragrance of her perfume. To my surprise, Mandy asked me, "Why are you undressing me with your eyes?" I was shocked by her statement and stuttered to get a complete statement out. She moved closer and whispered, "Are you a dog like your grandfather? Reverend Gould loves to chase women!" She then told me, "You are handsome, just like your grandfather."

I started blushing as I had never experienced a young lady being so direct with me before. But then again, I had never been exposed to young ladies from the city. Because it was getting dark, Mandy started walking home and looking back at me, laughing. I was stunned.

After I had stayed with my grandparents for around forty-five days, my mother called and told me, "Bring your ass home and get a job!" My sixteenth birthday was approaching, and I could legally get a full-time summer job in North Carolina. My mother had already found a job for me through a friend. It was doing heavy manual labor, working on the railroad.

TRACKS OF OUR TEARS

That evening, I told Mandy, "I am catching the bus this weekend to go back to North Carolina." We embraced, kissed, and cried.

The next day, Mandy came over to the house and gave me a new 45 record by Smokey Robinson and the Miracles with the song titled "The Tracks of My Tears." She autographed the record and dedicated the song to me. She then kissed me and walked away crying. I felt helpless and could not hold back my tears.

SHOPPING FOR SCHOOL CLOTHES WITH GRANDMOTHER GOULD

Since my birthday was approaching, Grandmother Gould asked me, "Would you like to go shopping for school clothes before leaving Newport News?" Of course, my quick response was "Yes!"

When we arrived at the men's store, Grandmother Gould advised me, "Do not select cheap clothes, because they wear out quickly."

She took charge and started selecting fashionable clothes for me. She bought me a full-length black leather coat, several expensive alpaca sweaters, button-down shirts, pants, and shoes. I hugged and thanked my grandmother repeatedly for being so nice to me for my upcoming birthday. I was now anxious for fall weather so I could show off my new wardrobe at school.

That weekend, as my grandparents were about to drive me uptown to catch the bus, Mandy ran over to the car and gave me a perfume-scented letter with her mailing address and telephone number and told me, "Stay in touch." Mandy walked slowly behind the car as we drove away, tears streaming down her face. I got on my knees in the back seat of the car, waved, and threw kisses until she vanished.

MY BUS RIDE TO NORTH CAROLINA

After I boarded the bus, I decided to eat one of the fried chicken sandwiches Grandmother Gould prepared for me. Grease was seeping through the wax paper and brown paper bag. After I finished eating the chicken sandwich, I drifted off to sleep with my head pressed against the bus window.

The bus made a stop in a small country town in Southern Virginia. As fate would have it, a lady with wide hips and a big butt got on the bus and sat in the aisle seat beside me. I could barely breathe as she mashed me against the bus window. To make matters worse, she fell asleep and leaned on me. When I arrived at my home bus station in Albemarle, North Carolina, I was tired. I felt like I had been in a prolonged wrestling match for seven hours.

CHAPTER 22

SUMMER JOBS AT THE AGE OF SIXTEEN

When I arrived home that weekend, my mother was anxious for me to start working on the railroad on Monday morning. She said, "You sat on your ass in Newport News this summer. Now it is time for you to make me some money." Once again, she used her famous quote, "By law I can take every dollar you earn while working until you reach the age of twenty-one." After hearing that statement, I went outside, climbed my favorite tall tree, and talked to the green tree leaves. They embraced and welcomed me back. I told them I had a wonderful time in Newport News. The green tree leaves advised me to cherish the wonderful summer memories as that was a snapshot of wonderful memories I would experience when I leave home.

By 7:00 a.m. on Monday, my mother dropped me off at the railroad construction site. A high school friend named Lester met me at the site and introduced me to the white supervisor, Mr. Task. He said, "Boy, this is hard work. It will take you a few days to adjust to the work and heat."

He then assigned me to work with a team of older black men. They looked at me, laughed, and said, "Slim, do you think you are strong enough to handle this hard work?" I boldly said, "Yes." They continued to laugh and make jokes about my slim body.

The team was responsible for removing and replacing heavy-duty old wood crossties and old railroad tracks with new ones. We used sledgehammers to nail down iron spikes into the wood to secure railroad tracks. Precision timing was crucial for the two-man team to accurately drive iron spikes into the wood using alternating blows. After I had observed their technique, they gave me a sledgehammer. After one hour, I fell down on one knee from heat exhaustion.

The white supervisor told me, "Go sit under the tree until after lunch."

During that time under the tree, I had a talk with myself. I said, "Kenneth, you have done harder work with Grandfather Little and your father." They often said, "To do hard work, you have to drink plenty of water and eat healthy meals to build strength." I concluded by saying to myself, "You are too stubborn to let these men see you fail. Kenneth, although you have a slim body, you are strong!"

At lunch, I ate a hearty meal and drank plenty of water.

After lunch, I was relentless in swinging the sledgehammer and nailing iron spikes into the wood. At the day's end, the team members told me, "We laughed at you this morning because we did not think you were going to make it. You are going to be a good worker!"

I give thanks to Grandfather Little and my father for strength and wisdom.

After two weeks on the job, I received my first paycheck, and my mother demanded that I give it to her. She stated again, "By law, I can take every dollar you earn until you reach the age of twenty-one!" She dropped me off at the house, drove to the store, and cashed my paycheck. From there, she went clothes and shoes shopping. When she returned, she gave me enough money to buy lunch at work for the next week. That weekend, she made me go to the golf course to caddie. I earned $8 that weekend, and she took that money too. My mother's greed for money made me feel like an indentured servant. Again, my father maintained a low profile.

NEW CLOTHES PURCHASED FOR ME BY GRANDMOTHER GOULD

One day, while I was at work on the railroad, my mother discovered the expensive clothes Grandmother Gould purchased for me in Newport News. She was very angry and told me, "I called your grandmother and told her to return your new clothes and send the cash refund to me." My mother said, "Your grandmother refused to return the clothes." My mother was livid! She then told me, "You do not deserve expensive clothes! Besides, it is your fault that I had a nervous breakdown!" I could not connect the dots between me having expensive clothes and me causing her to have a nervous breakdown. Go figure!

Surprisingly, my mother did not destroy my clothes. I did occasionally smell her scent in my expensive sweaters that she wore during the day. I had to put them in the cleaners to get rid of her scent. At this stage of my life, I was firmly convinced my mother's love of money was linked to her untreated mental health condition.

SCHOOL BUS DRIVER

During that summer, at the age of sixteen, I could get my learner's permit and, eventually, my driver's license. I developed a strategy to get my driver's license. I told my mother I wanted to be a school bus driver in the fall and earn $30 per month. Appealing to her greed for money paid off. I successfully passed the driver's permit test and subsequently passed the state driver's license and school bus driver's test. However, my being a school bus driver gave me status in the community.

Mr. Black, the West Badin School principal, selected me to be the new bus driver that fall. Of course, my mother took my $30 paycheck each month and cashed it. And following her traditional behavior, she spent my money on her new clothes and shoes.

FALL OF 1965

On the first day of school, my emotions stirred, and my heart raced when I saw Malinda. Over the summer months, she had blossomed. Malinda was increasingly more stunning, beautiful, and appealing. When she was in my presence, my eyes stayed fixed on her. My heart yearned for my lost love.

I did; however, continue to communicate with Mandy in Newport News, Virginia. As time went by, our communication hit a downward spiral. I soon mentally developed a long-distance love equation—that is, lovers' long time apart plus lovers' long distance apart equal zero love (long time + long distance = zero love). Throughout my love life experiences, this equation has been tried and tested a few times, each time yielding zero love. Love just faded away or I was replaced by someone new.

ELEVENTH GRADE, 1965

Ms. Miller was my eleventh-grade homeroom teacher. I was enrolled in several of her classes. She told me one day, "I want you to perform up to your full potential in school." I took her advice and started performing better in school. My parents were surprised when they saw good grades on my report card again.

It was my mother and father's desire for me to drop out of high school or graduate and get a blue-collar job. Making a career as a blue-collar worker is an honest way to make a living. I don't knock blue-collar work, especially if that's what a person wants to do. My father always boasted, "You have to get your hands dirty to make good money." My mother thought I would get a blue-collar job, stay at home, and continue to give her my hard-earned money. Wrong! I wanted to continue my education and eventually get a good-paying white-collar job. Their desires did not fit into my dreams and visions for a better life

My secret desire was to graduate from high school the following year, leave home immediately, and start fulfilling my dreams and visions. These dreams and visions were locked into my mind, soul, and spirit.

MR. PIMP'S BOOTY CALL

One night around 10:00 p.m., I heard my father leave home for work at Alcoa. He was on the 11:00 p.m. to 7:00 a.m. shift. Shortly after 11:00 p.m., I heard a male's voice in my mother's bedroom. It was Mr. Pimp. I could hear them having sex. After they finished having sex, they laughed and talked. My bedroom was right across the hall.

My first thought was to get out of bed, turn on my mother's bedroom light, and threaten to tell my father about Mr. Pimp being in the house. Then my common sense kicked in. I did not want to face my mother's subsequent mean fury.

His coming into my father's house to have sex with my mother took my dislike for Mr. Pimp to a new low. He totally disrespected my father, his family, and his house. I was so disgusted with Mr. Pimp and my mother.

WEARING TO SCHOOL THE NEW CLOTHES GRANDMOTHER GOULD PURCHASED

The weather was getting cooler, and it was finally time for me to make my debut at school wearing my new clothes, shoes, and black leather coat. It was uplifting for me to receive positive remarks from my classmates regarding my new wardrobe. Some young ladies did a double take and closely checked me out when I walked down the hall or entered classrooms. The attention I received at school made my outside appearance seem happy. However, I felt tormented inside because of unrest at home.

Some days after school, when I finished driving my school bus route, I parked the bus in our driveway. Sometimes I stayed on the bus for hours to avoid facing my mother's verbal abuse. I pretended to clean the school bus. Since my green tree leaves had vanished for the fall and winter, I sat on the warm bus and pondered on my future dreams and visions.

In a surprise move one day, Mr. Black, West Badin School's principal, announced, "If any West Badin students want to transfer to North Stanly High School (all white segregated school), they should complete transfer paperwork and have it signed by their parents." Student transfers went into effect during the 1965–1966 school year.

Because of the historic legal case Brown v. Board of Education and the new civil rights laws, public schools were mandated to integrate. Just to be adventurous, I decided to transfer to North Stanly High School my senior year (twelfth grade). Mr. Black, West Badin's principal, selected me to be a bus driver to transport students (ninth through twelfth grades) to North Stanly High School, located in New London, North Carolina. Numerous other students decided to transfer as well.

SUMMER JOBS AT THE AGE OF SEVENTEEN

Shortly after school closed for the summer, one day I was waiting to caddie at the golf course. The golf pro suddenly opened the back window of the pro shop and said, "Kenneth, meet me around front." He offered me a full-time summer job, working forty hours per week as a greens-keeper. He also promised to let me caddie on weekends. He kept his promise, and I worked seven days a week that summer.

Securing my summer jobs was perfect timing, as my family was struggling financially. My father was again laid off by Alcoa. He was hitting dead ends searching for a job. My parents used my summer income to support our household and to save money to purchase a new car.

Our family car was old. It sputtered each time my father hit the accelerator and discharged long streams of white smoke from the car's exhaust pipe. Seeing the car discharge smoke caused my classmates to laugh. Because of the car's dense white smoke, they nicknamed our old car the Mosquito Killer. As fate would have it, my father eventually found a construction job. Money from his new job and money from my summer jobs enabled my parents to purchase a new car.

STRANGE TWIST OF FATE

That fall, another strange twist of fate happened. Alcoa had installed computers systems in the pot room, where black males worked. Computers reduced guesswork involved in melting iron ore. Laid-off workers were now required to pass a simple math test to be rehired by Alcoa.

My father learned through some rehired workers that Mr.

Pimp had tutored them in math. They passed Alcoa's simple math test and were rehired by Alcoa. Strangely enough, my father reached out to Mr. Pimp and went to his house for math tutoring. With Mr. Pimp's tutoring, my father passed the math test and was rehired by Alcoa.

At first, it was hard for me to wrap my mind around the math tutoring situation between Mr. Pimp and my father. The life lesson for me was my father's humility. He desperately wanted to support his family. I had to commend my father for reaching out to a man who had been dating his wife (my mother) for years. I also had to respect Mr. Pimp's willingness to tutor my father.

This strange twist of fate was that two men who were not friends came together in peace. I had already heard through Badin gossip that Mr. Pimp tutored my father in math. One day, my father decided to tell me, "Mr. Pimp tutored me in math and helped me get my job back at Alcoa." I pretended to be stunned.

Another strange twist, my mother never uttered a word about Mr. Pimp tutoring my father. However, she continued to date Mr. Pimp. I guess my mother's sex was Mr. Pimp's reward for helping my father secure his job at Alcoa. My father continued to physically abuse my mother each time he caught her out on dates with Mr. Pimp. I often wondered how my mother tolerated my father's brutal ass-whippings. She ended up with black eyes and swollen lips. Did my mother have a fetish? Did she enjoy the brutal ass-whippings? This unrest really became the norm in our household.

CHAPTER 23

INTEGRATING NORTH STANLY HIGH SCHOOL

AUGUST 1965

In August 1965, I was a senior in high school. I and students on my bus were riding an emotional roller coaster. It was our first day arriving and integrating at North Stanly High School (previously, only white students attended). We received a quiet but peaceful reception as we walked through the school's main entrance. You could hear a pin drop as hundreds of white students stared at us while they leaned against the walls. Several white males who worked at the golf course spoke to me as I walked down the hall. The school principal, Mr. White, greeted and assigned us to our respective homerooms.

On some occasions, white students posted on the school's walls, "The Ku Klux Klan members are watching you." They were referring to black students. In turn, we responded by writing, "The NAACP is too!" On one occasion, I got into an argument with a white male student; he called me the N word and took off running into a teacher's classroom. When I looked at him in the classroom, his face was red and his body trembled with fear. To avoid getting in trouble, I just walked away.

One month later, Mr. White and the county bus supervisor did a surprise bus inspection. I was selected as the school's bus driver of the month due to a safe driving record and bus cleanliness. I received recognition with a write-up in the local newspaper, the Stanly County News and Press. But my mother was not impressed with my recognition. She asked, "Does money come with the recognition?" I sadly answered, "No!" I thought she would be proud of me.

NEW YOUNG LADY

Eventually, I met and dated a beautiful young lady named Ciara Burton. She lived in New London. Ciara was a very nice young lady. Her parents imposed a strict curfew on the time I could visit her at home. I often caught a ride to visit her with my friend John. He was my former West Badin classmate and was dating Ciara's cousin, who lived nearby.

Ciara was also a transfer student who once rode the school bus from New London to a segregated high school in Albemarle (formerly known as Kingsville School). Kingsville School had a similar school structure as West Badin School, with elementary, middle, and high school students on one campus. Ciara's travel time to school was greatly reduced from one hour to less than thirty minutes during her junior year at North Stanly High School. During my senior year at North Stanly High, my affection for Ciara grew stronger.

I felt so bad. I could not let my affection for Ciara derail my future. I planned to immediately move away from New London after high school graduation. I had a tight grasp on my future visions and dreams for a better life.

HIGH SCHOOL GRADUATION

In June 1966, I graduated from high school. Grandfather and Grandmother Gould drove down to New London the day after I graduated to take me back to Newport News, Virginia, to live with them. What a happy day!

Before leaving New London, early that morning, I climbed my tall tree to say goodbye to the green tree leaves. I thanked them for their counsel, encouragement, and support for me from third through twelfth grades in school. They advised me to stay strong and stay focused on my dreams and visions. I waved goodbye to them as I got into the back seat of my grandparents' car. As we drove away from my house, I looked straight ahead and refused to look back. I was ready to turn the page and start a new CHAPTER of my life in Newport News, Virginia. In my mind, this was the end of an emotional legacy for me—thank the Lord!

While driving to Newport News, Grandfather Gould decided to stop in High Point, North Carolina, to visit his cousin named Ethel. She made money selling liquor as a bootlegger. She had a beautiful large house and a luxury car. After we entered the house, Grandfather Gould whispered to Ethel, and they disappeared into the kitchen. Cousin Ethel came back into the living room to talk to Grandmother Gould and me.

After about an hour, Grandmother Gould told me to go into the kitchen to check on my grandfather. A pint jar of white corn liquor was empty, and he had passed out drunk sitting at the kitchen table. I woke him up, and he said, "Grandboy, I am not feeling well. Help me walk to the car." As I escorted him to the car, he gave me the car keys and asked me to drive to Newport News. I put him in the car's back seat, and he fell asleep immediately. Grandmother Gould was furious and fussed at least an hour about my grandfather being drunk before she fell asleep. I woke them up when we arrived home in Newport News.

CHAPTER 24

MY NEW LIFE IN NEWPORT NEWS, VIRGINIA

Every morning, I woke up with a smile on my face as I now lived in a peaceful environment. Grandfather Gould got me a job working as a sheet metal worker in the Newport News Shipyard. I could not start working for several weeks as I was still seventeen years old.

The day I turned eighteen in July, I reported for work. I was issued a construction hard hat and safety eyeglasses. I was assigned to work with a certified sheet metal mechanic named Mr. Jones. He sent me to the shipyard's shoe store to buy a pair of steel-toe safety shoes. Money was deducted from my weekly paycheck to pay for the shoes. I also wore work gloves every day as I refused to get my hands dirty and develop a lot of calluses. I viewed my blue-collar job as a stepping stone toward greater things in the future. I was happy.

Mr. Jones and I removed old air ventilation on ships, aircraft carriers, and submarines and installed new ventilation. These vessels were headed to Vietnam to support American and South Vietnamese troops in the Vietnam conflict. The combat mission was labeled as a conflict because the president and US Congress never declared war on North Vietnam.

I worked from 7:00 a.m. to 4:00 p.m. Monday through Friday. Sometimes I was required to work overtime hours. The work was hard and dirty. My work history with Grandfather Little and my father had prepared me for hard work. I was happy to have steady income.

Grandfather Gould charged me $10 per week for room and board. Looking back, starting back to when I was at the age of eight, Grandfather Little had already prepared me for this time, paying rent when living in someone's house. I rode the city bus to and from work. Most of the time, I purchased my meals at local restaurants. It was great living an independent life. Of course, my mother called and demanded that I send her money. As always, she quoted her familiar slogan, "I can take every dollar you earn until you are at the age of twenty-one!"

It really did not take me long to realize that sending me to live in Newport News with my grandparents was my mother's subtle attempt to continue to control my life and money. Deep down inside, I knew moving to Newport News was just a temporary layover. It was the first step to pursuing my lifelong dreams and visions.

REGISTER WITH LOCAL MILITARY DRAFT BOARD IN ALBEMARLE, NORTH CAROLINA

My mother called me one afternoon after work. She said, "You received a letter from the local military draft board in Albemarle, North Carolina." Federal law required eighteen-year-old males to register with their local draft board. The law stressed failure to do so could lead to time in prison.

I asked and secured time off work from my supervisor to go to North Carolina to register with the local draft board. I caught the bus late on a Thursday night from Newport News and arrived midmorning on Friday in Albemarle, North Carolina. I walked to a segregated restaurant and ate breakfast. Afterward, I walked to the local draft board and completed registration paperwork. I then called my father and asked him to pick me up in Albemarle. He arrived about thirty minutes later.

Since my father had been drafted in the army during World War II, he warned me to take local draft board's letters seriously. He mentioned that during World War II, some of his friends ignored their draft letters and ended up in prison. My father instilled in me that every young man should serve in the military to support his country.

The Vietnam conflict was growing at a steady pace, and the military needed more military personnel. It was inevitable; local draft board staff (all-white staff) was drafting mostly young black males starting in 1966. While at home, I called a few of my former West Badin School classmates and found out they had already received draft notices and were soon scheduled to be inducted into the army or marines. They advised me the local draft board was granting waivers to males who were enrolled in college.

CHAPTER 25

PURSUING MY DREAMS AND VISIONS

I felt happy when I returned to Newport News and blessed to have a decent-paying blue-collar job. But my real dreams and visions were to get a college education and eventually secure a higher-paying white-collar job.

Every afternoon, while riding the city bus home, I noticed students coming and going at a small business school, former Peninsula Business College (PBC). It was located on Jefferson Avenue in Newport News. One afternoon, I decided to get off the bus near the school. I was dirty and smelly but decided to go inside to talk to a PBC adviser.

She advised me that PBC offered a two-year business program. Most of the students who graduated from PBC transferred their PBC school credits to four-year colleges or secured a white-collar job with the federal government.

There were numerous federal military facilities near Newport News. These facilities included Fort Eustis, Virginia; Hampton, Virginia; Norfolk, Virginia; and Portsmouth, Virginia. Some students moved to Washington, DC, to get white-collar jobs, as the pay grade structure was higher. I was impressed with PBC's curriculum and returned on Friday (payday) to make a cash deposit on tuition.

ENROLLED IN BUSINESS SCHOOL

The PBC adviser informed me of the strict dress code for students. School policies required men to wear dress shirts and neckties to class. This was to prepare male students for the professional business world. With that in mind, I walked ten blocks to the most fashionable men's store in Newport News. I used their layaway plan to buy business attire, such as business suits, sports coats, shoes, button-down shirts, and ties. When school started in September, I had a very stylish wardrobe.

To my surprise, I turned a few ladies' heads when I walked to school. Those days, I felt like I was living a double life. I was a blue-collar worker during the day and dressed like a white-collar worker at night school. I enrolled in math, typing, English, accounting, and other classes. I was laying the foundation to pursue my dreams and vision of a better life. I would be elated if my green tree leaves in North Carolina could see and talk to me now. I continued to feel Skip's loving spirit following me around Newport News. I was overflowing with happiness.

I soon received my draft notice from the local draft board (all-white staff) in Albemarle, North Carolina. I took the notice to my PBC adviser and asked her to type a letter for me to send to the local draft board in Albemarle, North Carolina, to inform the staff that I was enrolled in college. The local draft board staff responded and granted me a waiver. I was happy, happy, happy!

SUMMER LOVE CONSUMMATED

One evening, I was home alone in the living room, studying for business classes. The front door screen was open to allow cool air to circulate throughout the house. The screen door was unlocked. I was startled when the screen door opened, and suddenly, Mandy was standing in the living room. She always had free rein to come and go at any time in my grandparents' house.

That evening, my grandparents were away from home. Compared to two summers ago, Mandy had matured into an attractive young lady. She stood around five feet five inches tall, with a gingerbread-colored skin complexion. I observed Mandy wearing a low-cut V-neck top and a short skirt, exposing her beautiful, shapely legs. The perfume she was wearing was breathtaking. She started flirting with me, and soon, hot romance filled the air in the living room. It really caught fire when we moved into my bedroom. I tuned her up as we lovingly embraced between the sheets.

Mandy went into my bedroom that evening full of innocence and walked out leaving her innocence behind. We had just consummated our love for each other. The next month, her menstrual cycle appeared on time; we were so happy that she was not pregnant. That day, I made a promise to myself to not engage in unprotected sex in the future. I went to the drugstore and bought a box of prophylactics. I hid them in my locked suitcase under the bed and put one in my wallet, in case of an emergency.

Mandy was in her senior year in high school, and her parents placed strict curfew hours on her. She was an honor student and wanted to attend a four-year college in North Carolina. Her father was a blue-collar worker at the shipyard, and her mother was a homemaker. They wanted a better life for Mandy.

CHAPTER 26

A NEW YOUNG LADY

One night, PBC's administrative secretary entered classrooms and announced the "Back-to-School Formal Dance." She said, "The dance is in two weeks, on a Saturday night in Hampton, Virginia, and would last from 10:00 p.m. to 2:00 a.m." I knew Mandy's parents would strongly object to her going to a dance and staying out that late. I decided to rent a tuxedo and catch a ride to the dance with a fellow classmate.

On Friday night, before the dance, a twenty-year-old young lady named Terri Jason approached me at school. Terri grew up in Newport News. She asked me, "Would you like to go to the dance with me?" Terri was very attractive and sexy. Her vibrant smile could light up a room. She was around five feet four inches tall, with a caramel skin complexion and light-brown hair and eyes, and she always wore stylish clothes. Terri was a senior at PBC.

I could not believe this attractive young lady was asking me to go to the dance with her. Being a shy eighteen-year-old country boy, I was at a loss for words for a few minutes and eventually mumbled, "I do not have a car." She then sarcastically said, "I did not ask you if you had a car! I asked if you wanted to go to the dance with me! I do not have a car either. I am riding with my girlfriend."

Feeling nervous and thinking she was way out of my league, I said, "I am already riding with John." And I refused her offer. Terri shook her head in disgust, turned, and walked away. She stopped abruptly and said, "Are you trying to play hard to get?" I responded very sheepishly and said "No." Deep down inside, I lacked confidence and knew I did not have experience in dealing with an older lady from the city.

BACK-TO-SCHOOL DANCE

When I arrived at the dance, Terri was the first person I saw sitting at a table near the building entrance. I tried to ignore Terri as I passed by her table, but she called out my name and said, "Ken, how are you?" Terri pointed me out to her friends sitting at her table. They looked, smiled, and waved at me. I smiled and waved to them. Based on my timid behavior, I am sure they viewed me as a shy country boy.

I was wearing stylish evening attire, but my stomach was bubbling from nervousness! I felt uncomfortable and needed a confidence booster.

MY DOUBLE SHOT OF SCOTCH LIQUOR

I went to the cash bar and ordered a double shot of scotch liquor on the rocks. This was the same drink the man in the line ahead of me ordered. I had never drunk this much liquor in my life, but this shy country boy wanted to come alive that night. In short, that double shot of scotch gave me a confidence booster, and I was ready to dance.

That double shot of scotch convinced me to go over to Terri's table. I gently touched her hand and asked, "Would you like to dance?" She got up and smiled at me as we walked onto the dance floor. We danced the night away on every upbeat, fast song the band played. Suddenly, the band slowed the pace and played a slow love song. I turned to walk off the dance floor. Terri grabbed my hand and asked, "Will you slow dance [slow drag] with me?" I had an immediate flashback to a house party I attended in high school. Teenagers laughed at me because I couldn't slow dance. I vowed to never make a fool of myself again trying to slow dance.

The scotch, or truth serum, overpowered my brain, and I told Terri, "I don't have the rhythm to slow dance." She smiled, wrapped her arms around me, and pulled me close and softly whispered in my ear, "Just follow my lead." The scotch made me say, "Okay!"

We danced slowly to a beautiful love song and held each other so tightly. We could feel the intense pounding of each other's heartbeats. The scotch then told me to take charge of the slow dance, as I had found my slow dance rhythm. Feeling a little nasty, I decided to add a few grinding moves to the slow dance, and she sheepishly rolled her caramel-colored eyes at me and slowly backed away.

As my confidence continued to build, I decided to steal a few kisses on Terri's jaw. The scotch then made me act boldly, and I cautiously moved closer and gave her a dry kiss on the lips. As I started to back away, Terri placed her hand behind my head and pulled me close and gave me a very romantic, passionate kiss. It felt like our tongues were in a tug-of-war. Terri's kisses were sweet as cakes Grandmother Little used to make. This slow dance was turning into a hot and steamy romance on the dance floor. I felt like I was moving fast, climbing the stairway to heaven.

ROOKIE SCOTCH LIQUOR DRINKER

I suddenly moved away from Terri's grasp as the taste of scotch and chicken wings with hot sauce moved from my stomach up to my throat and was about to emerge from my mouth. I left Terri on the dance floor and ran quickly toward the men's restroom. The door was locked, so I ran outside. All the food and drink I consumed that night was now on the ground in front of the building. I was so sick, leaning against the building.

Terri came outside with wet paper towels and wiped my mouth and face. She then sat me down on the steps and placed my head on her shoulder. I repeatedly said, "I'm so sorry about the accident!"

She said, "Be quiet," and placed my head on her shoulder and softly rubbed my face and head. I reeked with the smell of "throw up," but it really did not seem to bother Terri.

We sat on the building steps for at least an hour, embracing each other. The only time she left my side was to go inside to get her coat. I offered her my tuxedo jacket, but she refused. That night, it was windy, with high tide coming in at Bay Shore Beach in Hampton, Virginia. Moisture from splashing beach water put a chill in the air. The school dance was sponsored in a building on Bay Shore Beach. The beach was still segregated in the late 1960s.

The school dance was over at 2:00 a.m. The adage "Time flies when you are having fun" was appropriate at the dance. I did not want to leave Terri's arms. John, my classmate, whom I rode with, gave me a few minutes to get a good-night kiss from Terri. As we drove away from the facility, I started throwing up again—it was all over the side of John's car. I offered him money to pay for car wash. But he refused to take the money. That night, I promised myself to never again drink a double shot of scotch on the rocks.

I COULD NOT BELIEVE MY EYES

That Sunday morning, I slept late, trying to recover from my scotch liquor hangover. Around noon, I got up, took a long hot shower, got dressed, and decided to go out to buy lunch at a restaurant on Jefferson Avenue. As I turned off Hampton Avenue and walked onto Jefferson Avenue, I looked up and saw a beautiful, smiling face. It was Terri. Feeling embarrassed, I immediately dropped my head.

As I walked toward Terri, I found $20 lying on the sidewalk in front of me. I picked it up, walked over to Terri, and apologized again for getting drunk the night before. She said, "Will you stop apologizing?" I then asked, "May I buy you lunch with the money I just found?" She accepted.

We sat in a Chinese restaurant and ate Yaka Mein (tomato-flavored noodles with sliced pork or chicken) and beef fried rice (the rice had a black color). These Chinese dishes had a unique but delicious flavor and could only be found in the Newport News and Hampton, Virginia, areas.

We sat in the restaurant, talked for hours, and shared personal background information. Before going our separate ways, Terri invited me to come to her house and meet her parents the next weekend. I smiled and said, "Yes!" I was happy as a dog in a meat market. I was thrilled to see Terri again.

MEETING TERRI'S MOTHER AND GRANDMOTHER

On the next Saturday evening, I walked to Terri's house. Her mother, Mrs. Jason, answered the door. We had a long talk while Terri was getting dressed. Mrs. Jason asked me a lot of probing questions about my background and future plans. I was very forthcoming in providing personal information. I also offered my grandparents' telephone number to allay Mrs. Jason's fears about me. I appreciated Terri's mother's concern about her daughter's welfare and safety.

Terri's mother was very attractive and smart, and I instantly summed her up as being a wonderful person. Mrs. Jason fit the description of a typical redbone, a nickname for light-skinned women of that era. She had very fair skin, keen facial features, and long black hair. Terri inherited her beauty from her mother.

I did not want Grandfather Gould to meet Mrs. Jason as he would have tried to date her. I was sad to learn that Terri's father had passed away several years earlier.

I heard slow footsteps coming down the stairs. It was an elderly lady, Terri's grandmother. She entered the living room and introduced herself to me as Ms. Bertha. She then said, "You are just a young boy! Yes, I called you a boy, because you are not a man yet! Just because you have a little hair on your face does not make you a man." I laughed and stood up to shake her hand, but instead, I decided to give her a hug. Ms. Bertha was fun loving and feisty. She was short with gray hair, with chocolate-colored skin. I instantly developed affection for Mrs. Jason and Ms. Bertha. Later that night, Terri gave me a good-night kiss at the front door and sent me on my way.

IS THIS RELATIONSHIP REAL?

Suddenly, I realized that I had thrown caution to the wind. I asked myself, "Is Terri playing with my emotions?" Common sense and fear kicked in, so I proceeded with caution.

I really wanted to consult with my green tree leaves in North Carolina to get their advice. Just then, I remembered my dog Skip's spirit was still watching over me. I said aloud, "Skip, please give me a sign that your spirit is still with me." I then heard a dog bark in the distance. I took the dog's bark as a sign from Skip and decided to stay the course in pursuing a relationship with Terri.

It was Sunday afternoon, and I was at home, trying to catch up on my school studies. I planned to call Terri later to ask her to go to the movies. I tried to strike a balance with work, school, and romance. I was determined to continue juggling these three important activities in my life. I had to remain steadfast in pursuing my longstanding dreams and visions for a better life.

Although I was only eighteen years old in chronological years, I felt like I was much older. This was because of demands on the life I had lived and dealing with my parents. I was glad that I could still love after seeing my parents' behavior toward each other.

MANDY'S VISIT

It dawned on me that Mandy's eighteenth birthday was in late October. I bought her a few of her favorite music records and a box of candy and took her to the movies. She was happy.

The next afternoon, unexpectedly, there was a knock on the door. It was Mandy. She came into the house with a very stern look on her face, which was unusual behavior for her. Normally, she was smiling, bubbly, and full of energy. I could tell something was bothering her. I asked, "Do you feel okay?" She said no. Mandy sat down on the living room sofa beside me and started crying. I got some tissue and wiped her tear stained face.

Between sniffles, she tried to talk. She finally gained her composure and asked me, "Do you remember what I asked you two summers ago?" She then said, "It was the first day I met you in Newport News."

Trying to avoid opening her floodgate of tears again, I gave her a safe answer. I said, "We talked about a lot of things that day."

Mandy paused for a minute and just stared at me. She then raised her voice and said, "I asked you if you were a dog like your grandfather. I also told you Reverend Gould loved to chase women!" Mandy then said, "Okay, let's fast-forward, are you a dog like your grandfather?" To sidestep the question, I politely asked her, "Please lower your voice," as Grandmother Gould was upstairs, reading the

Bible to Grandfather Gould.

I wiped more tears from her face, pulled her close, and kissed her. As our body temperatures rose, I ran quickly into my bedroom and got a prophylactic. I had stocked up on prophylactics as I did not want to get anyone pregnant, especially Mandy.

Our passionate kisses led us to quietly and passionately making love on the couch in my grandparents' living room. Afterward, Mandy combed her hair and fixed her clothes. She then told me, "I hope you enjoy your relationships with Terri and other women." As Mandy walked toward the front door, she pointed toward upstairs and quietly said, "You're a dog, just like your grandfather!"

I stood there like a deer staring into car headlights. Then a sarcastic thought crossed my mind. I wondered why she continued to come into the doghouse. Bowwow!

For a moment, I thought about Mandy labeling me as a dog like my grandfather. Her statement also triggered thoughts of my mother's extramarital affairs. I concluded that I could no longer cast stones at my grandfather or my mother as I was a part of their bloodline. As the old saying goes, "The apple does not fall too far from the tree!"

MY MOVIE DATE WITH TERRI

Later that evening, I called and asked Terri to go to the movies. After I showered and got dressed in my stylish clothes and spit-shined shoes, I splashed on expensive men's Jade East cologne. I applied thick hair grease to make sure I had lots of waves in my hair, and lastly, I put on the long black leather coat Grandmother Gould bought me two summers ago. I was ready to make a fashion statement on my date with Terri.

As I walked out the door, I saw Mandy standing on her front porch. I waved as I walked by, and she responded, "Have fun on your date with Terri, Reverend Gould Jr.!" We laughed out loud.

TERRI'S COUSIN PUT ME ON BLAST

When I arrived at Terri's house, her cousin Marilyn was sitting in the living room. Terri introduced us. Marilyn said, "I have been dying to meet you! I am a senior in high school, and Mandy and I are in the same honors program for seniors."

This really connected the dots for me regarding Mandy's behavior. Marilyn was feeding Mandy information about me and Terri. Terri just stared at me and waited for my reaction to her cousin's statement. I ignored Marilyn's comment about Mandy, and I calmly asked Terri, "Are you ready to go to the movies?" As we walked out the door, I turned and said, "Nice meeting you, Marilyn." Marilyn could tell there was no sincerity in my parting comment to her. She just chuckled.

SCHOOL NIGHTS

On school nights, I rushed home from work to eat, shower, and get dressed for school. My stress faded away when I met Terri on the corner of Hampton Avenue and Jefferson Avenue so we could walk to school together. During bad weather, we rode the city bus together.

Terri had an A average in school and was always willing to tutor me in accounting. This class was a real challenge for me. She was great at explaining accounting fundamentals. Fortunately for me, the tutoring sessions gave me more time with her.

Because Terri and I spent so much time together—before, during, and after school—our classmates assumed we were a loving couple. We had not put a label on our relationship, and I could only speak for myself when I say I was growing madly in love with Terri.

I treasured the blissful moments I spent with her. When the time was right, I was going to ask her if we could define our relationship. Were we just friends? But for now, I decided to cruise along, enjoy the smooth sail, and not rock the boat.

THANKSGIVING DAY DINNER

It was late November, and the weather was bitterly cold. The moisture from the nearby James River put a frigid chill in the air. Leaves had fallen from the few trees by our house on Hampton Avenue. I thought about my green tree leaves in North Carolina, as they were now in hibernation. I really missed them and their counsel.

One night after school, Terri asked, "What are your plans for Thanksgiving?" I told her I would probably pick up some Chinese food and take it home. Terri then said, "My mother and grandmother told me to invite you to Thanksgiving dinner." I said, "Okay, I will join your family for dinner under one condition. I will buy the Thanksgiving turkey." Terri gave me some push-back on my suggestion but finally agreed.

The next afternoon, I went to the grocery store and bought a twenty-pound turkey and took it to Terri's house. This was Grandfather Little's training; he did not like deadbeats (people who always wanted something for nothing). I could not, in good conscience, sit down at their table without contributing to Thanksgiving dinner.

The house was full of loud music and laughter. I ate like a pig, as the food and desserts were delicious. I went home late from Terri's house that night as I did not have to work the next day. I really enjoyed the peaceful and harmonious environment at Terri's house.

CONSUMMATED OUR LOVE ON THANKSGIVING DAY WEEKEND

Terri and I were together every day and night during Thanksgiving weekend. Early on Sunday morning on Thanksgiving weekend, Terri called and asked, "Will you join me for breakfast at my house this morning?" Her mother and grandmother were away at church. When I walked into the house, she was playing slow dance songs on the stereo (record player). She took my coat and said, "Let's slow dance!" Without a drink of scotch liquor, I took charge and led the dance. As we were kissing, bumping, and grinding, I started feeling frisky. As I rubbed her sexy body, I discovered that she was not wearing a bra or panties. I started sweating profusely. My entire body was throbbing. She melted like butter in my arms. I had waited months for this blissful moment.

I stopped dancing and led her over to the couch. As I went into my wallet to secure a prophylactic, she got completely undressed. I took a moment to admire her beautiful, shapely naked body as it was like classic art. My mind took a snapshot of her beautiful body lying sprawled on the couch. This was the moment I had looked forward to. She kept me waiting for months. Our bodies blended as one as we floated away in ecstasy. She was a very passionate lover, and I was on my way, climbing the stairway to heaven.

I did not want that blissful moment to end, but her mother and grandmother were due to come home from church very soon. Terri rearranged the pillows on the couch to make it look neat again. She opened the door, gave me a kiss, and said, "Call me later." Terri grabbed her clothes and dashed upstairs to take a shower.

I walked along a back street to avoid seeing her mother and grandmother. I got lost walking home as my mind was in a daze thinking about my beautiful romance with Terri. I wondered if this romance consummated our love for each other. At least it did for me—I was ready for a repeat!

As I walked down the sidewalk toward my house after being with Terri, I felt the sidewalk moving under my feet. As I walked past Mandy's house, I heard a knock from her bedroom window. She threw me a kiss in passing, and I did the same. Mandy's action made me drop my head in shame. Did the dog develop a conscience?

CHAPTER 27

NEXT-DOOR NEIGHBOR'S LOVE STORY

I never introduced myself to our next-door neighbor. In fact, I never knew her name. She lived a very secluded life, rarely seen in public.

That night, when I returned home from Terri's house, I heard loud music coming from the next-door neighbor's house. I stood on our porch for a while, listening to her play this beautiful love song repeatedly. Lyrics in the song by William Bell said, "Every day will be like a holiday when my baby, when my baby comes home!"

On my way to work the next morning, she was still playing the same song. That afternoon, when I returned home from work, she was still playing the same song. As I was leaving home to go to school, she came out on the porch to get mail out of the mailbox.

I spoke and said, "You really love that song!" She smiled and said, "My husband is on his way home from Vietnam. I am going to play this song until he comes home." I was deeply touched by her response.

A few days later, while retrieving mail from our mailbox, I

looked up and saw a soldier in uniform walking down the sidewalk near our house. I waved and said, "Welcome home, soldier!"

He smiled and said, "Thank you!"

As he turned from the sidewalk to enter their house, his wife ran out the house, leaped into his arms, and kissed him passionately. The love song was still playing loudly in the background.

What a happy ending and a new beginning!

CHAPTER 28

GRANDMOTHER GOULD GOES TO NORTH CAROLINA FOR CHRISTMAS

GRANDFATHER GOULD'S CHRISTMAS PARTY AT THE HOUSE

Grandmother Gould rode the bus to New London, North Carolina, to visit my parents and her relatives. While Grandmother Gould was in North Carolina with my mother and father, Grandfather Gould stayed home in Newport News. One evening, I came home early to shower and change clothes as Terri and I were going to a dance later that night. As I walked into the house, I heard loud gospel music playing and loud laughter coming from the kitchen. I was curious as to what was going on in the house.

When I walked into the kitchen, I noticed the kitchen table was filled with a large basket of fried chicken and biscuits and about five different bottles of liquor, such as scotch, gin, bourbon, rum, and vodka. Grandfather Gould was shocked to see me. He stuttered and finally got some words out of his mouth and said, "Grandboy, would you like some chicken and biscuits?" I smiled and said, "No, thanks!"

After a few seconds of silence, Grandfather Gould said, "These are some of my church members." He introduced me to each one. There were three men sitting at the table and my grandfather. There were also four redbone women sitting at the table.

One lady stared at me for a few minutes and said, "I know your face. You come into my restaurant to eat."

I said, "Yes" and complimented her on serving delicious soul food at her restaurant. To be respectful to the adults, I said, "It was nice to meet everyone." I then excused myself to get ready for my date with Terri.

GRANDFATHER GOULD'S NUDE SHOW ON HAMPTON AVENUE

The next afternoon, I was walking out of the house when Brandy, a young lady who lived across the street, called me and said, "Come over to my house for a minute." Brandy laughed out of control. She then asked, "Where is your grandmother?" I responded, "She is in North Carolina, why do you ask?" After gaining her composure, she screamed out, "Reverend Gould put on a show for the neighbors last night! He was laughing, running around naked, and chasing a naked light-skinned woman through the house. Most of the nearby neighbors came out on the sidewalk to watch your grandfather and laughed out of control."

Brandy then told me, "Tell your grandfather to close the door and windows the next time he has a nude party!" She added, "Our nosey neighbors will tell Mrs. Gould what happened in her house while she was away in North Carolina."

Brandy then added, "One Sunday, I was walking to the park

to see a live band playing music when I saw your grandfather's car. I noticed an apartment with the door and windows wide open and was shocked to see your grandfather naked and chasing a naked light-skinned lady around the apartment! When he finally noticed me standing outside, looking at him, he came to the door and shouted, Girl, you better go on back to Hampton Avenue and mind your own business!'" She said, "I told him, I am going to tell Mrs. Gould I saw you over here!" She continued to laugh so hard until tears started flowing down her face.

Just to shock her, I said, "Brandy, are you turned on when you see my naked grandfather?" She stopped laughing and rolled her eyes at me. Brandy's comeback was "Mandy told me that you're a dog just like your grandfather!" I laughed and turned to walk away and jokingly said, "You better stop lusting after my grandfather, or I will tell my grandmother!" (We both laughed as I walked away.)

GRANDMOTHER GOULD RETURNS HOME

Grandmother Gould told me that she had the time of her life visiting and talking with relatives about the good old days. She also asserted that she was happy to come back home to Newport News. As Grandmother Gould was telling me about her visit, she suddenly had a sad look on her face. I quickly asked her, "Why are you suddenly so sad?"

She responded, "I am sad because after I told your mother I was ready to retire, she volunteered to take me to Social Security Administration to apply for benefits. Your mother then insisted that I give her a portion of my benefits each month because she took me to apply for benefits."

GRANDMOTHER GOULD'S SOCIAL SECURITY RETIREMENT BENEFITS

My grandmother said, "When we returned home, your mother said to me, 'I helped you get the money because I am smart.'" My mother then demanded that my grandmother give her half of her Social Security back pay and demanded half of her monthly Social Security check. Grandmother Gould said my mother only wanted cash money mailed to her. My grandmother was concerned that my mother was that greedy for money. After listening to my grandmother, all I could do was hang my head in disgust. I thought I was the only person my mother strongly demanded money from.

Suddenly, a strange thought popped into my head. Just before I moved to Newport News with my grandparents, my mother and father had a heated argument regarding one $300 telephone call. My father was angry because he had to pay the telephone bill. He asked my mother, "What the hell were you and your mother talking about on the telephone for eight hours?" My mother replied, "I cursed at my mother for eight hours about the mean treatment I endured from childhood until I left home." In a very angry voice, my father said, "Next time, you should write her a letter! It will cost less money!"

The telephone situation helped me connect the dots. My mother made my grandmother feel guilty about her childhood. That was why my grandmother agreed to send my mother money.

My mother called Grandmother Gould at least two or three times per week to find out the status of the Social Security back pay. My grandmother became really annoyed with my mother. When the Social Security back pay arrived, Grandmother Gould went to the bank and cashed the check. She gave me money to purchase a money order and asked me to mail it to my mother. The next time my mother called, she told my grandmother she received the money order. She then asked, "When will I receive half of your monthly Social Security check?" My grandmother hung up the telephone in disgust.

Each month thereafter, when my grandmother received her monthly Social Security check, she asked me to mail cash money to my mother. Was that greed or what?

CHAPTER 29

CHRISTMAS IN NORTH CAROLINA

I rode the bus to North Carolina to visit family and friends. My father could not pick me up from the bus station because he was working at Alcoa. I caught a taxicab from Albemarle to our house in New London. When I arrived at the house, I immediately gave my mother some money as a Christmas gift to put her in a good mood. It worked; she even offered to let me drive the family car. This was the car I helped them purchase when I was fifteen.

Because of working at Alcoa again, my father now owned a new pickup truck. The truck became his primary means of transportation for getting to work, hauling pigs to market to sell, and going hunting.

I walked outside the house and looked up at my barren tall tree—all my green tree leaves were hibernating. I missed talking to my green tree leaves. I just wanted to tell them that I was pursuing happiness in Newport News.

CHRISTMAS DAY WITH THE LITTLE FAMILY

On Christmas day, I drove the family car to Mount Gilead to see the Little family. I was eighteen, but after I entered the house, my mind reverted to the time when I was eight. I hugged my Grandmother Little, Grandfather Little, and Aunt Ellen. I felt love circulating throughout the living room. I gave everyone money as a Christmas gift.

This eighteen-year-old, now mentally aged eight, stood in the living room with tears in his eyes. These were tears of joy. I quietly reflected on the fond memories I had with the Little family. Their love and guidance brought stability and peace to my life while I was living with them. As I grew older and matured, I knew that when I bought a house, it would be filled with love, peace, and happiness. Love that filled the Little family's household served as a role model for Kenneth Leon Little's future home.

After I gained my composure, I grabbed a straight-back chair and sat close to my grandmother near the fire place. She had a big dip of Old Navy snuff in her bottom lip. We talked at length about my new life in Newport News. She concluded by saying, "You be a good boy, respect and treat people right, and the Lord will bless you!" She always wanted me to be a good person.

Grandfather Little didn't have much to say; he just sat in his chair, smiling. Before leaving, he said his famous words to me. "Boy, I taught you how to be a man." I owe Grandfather Little a debt of gratitude as he taught me how to be a man and how to laugh. As I drove away from the house, tears streamed down my face again. Fond memories of love and happiness with my grandparents and Aunt Ellen triggered tears of joy again.

On Christmas night, I visited some former classmates and stopped by a few house parties. A lot of my black male classmates had already been drafted into the US Army, and others had received draft notices from the local draft board. Local draft board staff was focusing primarily on West Badin's black males to fill their draft quotas. I felt somewhat secure, as they granted me a waiver for being in school.

MISSING MY NEW LIFE IN NEWPORT NEWS, VIRGINIA

My body was in North Carolina, but my mind was in Newport News. I called Terri on Christmas night to wish her a merry Christmas and gave her the time my bus would arrive in Newport News the next evening. She said, "I will be waiting for you at the bus station." When I got off the bus, I picked her up in my arms and started swinging her around and kissing her passionately.

CHRISTMAS GIFT FOR MANDY

Mandy and her family celebrated Christmas in North Carolina. I bought music records for Mandy as a Christmas gift because she loved music. Mandy was delighted to receive her records. She started playing the music while I was at their house. She sat down on the couch close to me and placed my hand on her leg. I always complimented her for having such beautiful, shapely legs.

Although fully dressed, she started rubbing her fully developed breasts on my arm. I got nervous because her monster-size father was at home. Her father was six feet five inches tall, muscular, and weighed around 250 pounds. I stood five feet eleven inches and weighed 145 pounds. Go figure!

She started laughing when I told her, "I am nervous being in your father's presence, and I have to go home." I really wanted to buy

Mandy some expensive Christmas gifts, but I did not want to raise her parents' suspicion about our intimate affairs.

As I walked out of her house, she gave me a good-night kiss and thanked me again for the Christmas gift. I ran down the steps at her house and leaped over the fence at my house. The way her father looked at me sent cold chills running up and down my spine! I believe he knew I was a dog like Grandfather Gould.

Speaking of being a dog, I ran into Mandy's father one afternoon in the local grocery store. He had a broad smile on his face as he pushed the grocery cart for an attractive young lady. She was walking close to him, holding his arm. He spoke and said, "Hey, Ken!" In turn, I said, "Hi, Mr. Bland!" I never mentioned a word to Mandy about seeing her father. That was grown folks' business.

I had issues of my own to contend with. I was in a love triangle, trying to love two women at the same time. I loved Mandy, and I loved Terri. Both were sexy, smart, and had beautiful personalities. Looking back, I think I loved Terri more as she could go to social events and could stay out late at night. Plus, we made passionate love quite often. This helped to put Terri in first place. This was an important love standard for an eighteen-year-old male.

CHAPTER 30

SPRING SEMESTER AT SCHOOL, 1967

I received good grades during the fall semester. My goal was to maintain the same performance level or better during the spring semester. I completed the 100-level classes and was now enrolled in level 110 business classes for the spring semester. I got a commitment from Terri to continue tutoring me during the spring semester.

TERRI MOVES TO WASHINGTON, DC, AND MANDY GOES TO COLLEGE

Terri and several ladies in her class passed the civil service exam and were offered jobs with the federal government in the Washington, DC, area. Terri moved to Washington, DC, in June 1967 to start her new job. I was so lonely without her.

In August 1967, Mandy moved away to start her freshman year at college in North Carolina. I missed her too.

CHAPTER 31

LETTERS FROM LOCAL DRAFT BOARD IN ALBEMARLE, NORTH CAROLINA

To add insult to injury, the local draft board sent me a letter that reversed my draft waiver status. They also advised me that a draft letter would be forthcoming. The United States continued to build up military personnel in South Vietnam. Some of my former classmates had completed either army or marines basic training, including military combat training, and were stationed in infantry units in South Vietnam.

Just to prove to myself that I could withstand any situation, I decided to talk to a marine recruiter. He really pumped me up about becoming a marine. He told me marine units in South Vietnam needed young marines to go out on search patrols to destroy the enemy. The recruiter told me to talk it over with my parents before making my decision. I still had this burning desire to serve in combat like my father.

TERRI'S FORMER HIGH SCHOOL CLASSMATE INJURED IN COMBAT IN VIETNAM CONFLICT

One Friday night, Terri rode the bus home to Newport News from Washington, DC. On Saturday afternoon, Terri and I went uptown to do some shopping. As we walked down the street, we ran into one of her former high school classmates. She was shocked to see him in a wheelchair. She emotionally asked him, "What happened to you?" He replied, "I was critically wounded in combat in South Vietnam while on patrol with other marines. Most of my buddies died, but I was fortunate to make it out of the jungle alive." Terri became emotional and told him, "Ken plans to sign up with the marines next week."

He looked at me and said, "Four months from now, you will be in combat, fighting in the jungles of South Vietnam." He further advised me that his combat training was for conventional warfare (fighting only happens on the front line); there was no front line in Vietnam. The enemy used guerrilla warfare tactics, meaning they could strike at any time or anywhere. It was hard to tell a South Vietnamese from a North Vietnamese (enemy). By this time, a flood of tears erupted from Terri's eyes.

Lastly, he said, "I did some research on the army before joining the marines, but I was hooked on that distinguished-looking marine corps dress uniform."

He added, "My research on the army revealed decent benefits. If you enlist for three years, the army will offer you a 120-day delayed-entry program (delay going into the military on active duty), plus you will have a chance to select your military occupation skill (MOS i.e., job). This will give you a chance to avoid being placed in an infantry unit. The biggest bonus is, you will be automatically promoted to the next grade after sixty days on active duty."

He then talked about being drafted into the army. "The draft only requires a soldier to serve a two-year enlistment, and a lot of the draftees are assigned to infantry units."

Most of my former West Badin School classmates were drafted and assigned to army or marine infantry units in Vietnam.

JOINING THE US ARMY

Terri became extremely emotional after talking with and seeing her former classmate who was then wheelchair bound. As we walked away, Terri jumped in front of me and pointed her finger at my face and said, "You are not joining the marines!" She asserted, "You are joining the army on the 120-day delayed program. Your business classes at PBC should help you qualify for an administrative position in the army. We are going to an army recruiter's office right now!"

By the time we arrived, the army recruiter's office was closed. Terri said, "Please promise me that you will stop by the army recruiter's office on Monday after work and enlist in the army." I promised.

She was very emotional and adamant about me not joining the marines. I had never seen her display this much emotions. On Sunday afternoon, she caught the bus back to Washington, DC. When she arrived home that night in Washington, DC, Terri called to specifically ask me to join the army. Again, I promised to stop by the army recruiter's office on Monday after work.

ARMY RECRUITER

I went to see the army recruiter on Monday afternoon after work. He gave me the same details regarding the army as Terri's former high school classmate did. I was impressed with the army's enlistment program, but I told the recruiter, "I want to finish this semester at school." I was also waiting to see if I would receive a draft notice from the local draft board in North Carolina.

LETTER FROM MY LOCAL DRAFT BOARD

In December, right after I finished the fall semester in business school, I received a "Greetings, this is Uncle Sam" letter from my local draft board in Albemarle, North Carolina. The letter noted that I had been drafted into the US Army and listed my reporting date of late December 1967 in North Carolina.

The next afternoon, Terri and I went to the army recruiter's office. I signed up for a three-year enlistment in the army. My guaranteed military occupational skill (MOS) would be clerk-typist. I also signed up for the army's delayed-entry program. Terri was happy that I signed up for the US Army. This also meant I would spend four additional months at home with Terri before going on active duty.

I decided not to enroll in business school for the 1968 spring semester.

CHAPTER 32

TERRI'S BOMBSHELL

On the way home from the army recruiter's office, Terri confessed, "I have a boyfriend on active duty in the marines." Her confession hit me like an atomic bomb. I was at a loss for words. After I regained my composure, I asked Terri, "Why are you just mentioning this to me?" Her response was "He was discharged from the marines a few days ago and came by my house last night." I was now very emotional and developed a lump in my throat. I then raised my voice and told her, "I am getting off the bus at the next stop. I need to cool off."

To my surprise, Terri jumped off the bus behind me in the frigid, twenty-five-degree weather. She ran behind me on the sidewalk and shouted, "I love you and want to spend the rest of my life with you!" I really hoped I made the right decision to stay with Terri. (Stayed tuned.)

ANOTHER BOMBSHELL

In January 1968, Terri told me, "I am experiencing morning sickness." I told her to calm down and gave her money to go to the doctor for a checkup. The pregnancy test came back positive. I had a flashback to the November night we had unprotected sex on the living room couch. This old expression applies: "What's done in the dark will come to the light." Our actions came back to haunt us. Oh, crap!

After work on Friday, I went to the credit union and withdrew $300. I used a pay telephone to call and asked Terri, "Please meet me uptown." When she arrived, I surprised her by taking her to a jewelry store to pick out an engagement ring. The ring she picked out had a unique shape and cost $250.

To me, that was a lot of money in the late 1960s. Terri was beaming with joy and accepted my proposal for marriage. I was nineteen, and Terri was twenty-one years old. She was positive that our marriage would work. Terri's mother and grandmother were happy about our engagement. They were always very nice to me.

MY BONEHEAD MOVE

Since I was leaving to join the army in April 1968, I wanted Terri to have a car to drive. I made a bonehead move. I was only nineteen years old. Since I was under the age of 21, I needed a parent to sign papers authorizing me to buy a car. I called home and asked my mother, "Will you or Daddy sign for me to get a car?" For a moment, she played mind games with me and acted like she was willing to sign for a car.

She then asked, "How much money have you saved?" I told her $500. She raised her voice in a crazy rage and said, "You better send that $500 home to me, or I will tell your grandfather to put your ass out of his house! Plus, by law, I can take every dollar you earn until you are twenty-one years old." I was really irritated hearing my mother use that same lame excuse to take my money.

I was angry at my mother's mean behavior regarding her

demand for my hard-earned $500. I decided to delay in sending my money to her. One evening after work, Grandfather Gould told me, "I received a telephone call from your mother. She said you have been disrespectful toward her. You cannot live in my house being disrespectful toward your mother."

She lied to my grandfather just to get my money. I sent the $500 to her just to keep the peace. Besides, I did not want to move away from Terri, as she was pregnant.

MY MOTHER'S MEAN TELEPHONE CALL TO TERRI'S MOTHER

One evening after work, I went to Terri's house and received an unusually chilly reception from Terri and her family. My immediate thought was, Terri told them that she was pregnant. Terri, her mother, and her grandmother sat down in the living room and stared at me for a few minutes. I was nervous and concerned about their behavior. Mrs. Jason spoke up and said, "Ken, I received a disturbing telephone call from your mother today." I responded by saying, "What? Not again!" I dropped my head as I was so embarrassed. I asked myself, how did my mother get Terri's mother's telephone number? I did not give her the number.

Mrs. Jason told me my mother said, "You have always been very disrespectful toward her, and you caused her to have a nervous break-down. Ken, she also told me to stop you from coming to my house. She made numerous negative comments about you."

At first, I dropped my head because I was so humiliated. Then I said to Mrs. Jason, Terri, and Ms. Bertha, "My mother is not telling the truth." I added, "My mother has a history of breaking up my relationships, starting in the tenth grade. All she ever wanted was for me to work and give her my hard-earned money!"

I stood up and walked toward the door and said, "I apologize for my mother's mean telephone call. Mrs. Jason, I have never disrespected you or your family, and again, I apologize for the telephone call. Just for the sake of peace and respect, I will not come to your house anymore."

That was one of the saddest days of my life. Their home was a happy place for me, and going there comforted me. I walked out of the house hanging my head in shame because of my mother's mean behavior.

I was within earshot when Terri yelled out and said, "Ken, please come back into the house!"

I paused for a moment, trying to decide if I wanted to face more embarrassment. As I walked back into the house, Mrs. Jason, Ms. Bertha, and Terri gave me a group hug. Mrs. Jason said, "You have always presented yourself to me and my family as a real gentleman, and you are always welcome in my home." Ms. Bertha smiled and told me, "I know you're a good boy." Lastly, Terri said, "I love you very much. Please stay!" I said, "I love you too!" I thanked the family at least a thousand times for allowing me to stay in their lives.

When I arrived home that night, I received a mean telephone call from my mother. I heard my grandmother eavesdropping on the upstairs telephone. My mother displayed her normal behavior. She cursed, belittled, and called me a dirty dog and accused me of aggravating her nervous condition. At the end of her conversation, she demanded that I mail my weekly paycheck to her. "Or I will tell your grandfather to put your ass out of his house."

I displayed my normal behavior. I did not say a word, just kept quiet. Experience had taught me that responding really pissed her off. From a young age, my thought had always been, why throw fuel on a burning flame? My father told me it takes two people to argue. Time and experience with my mother forced me to adopt his philosophy.

My mother called again later that night, and my grandmother answered the telephone. I heard them arguing, so I decided to eavesdrop on the downstairs telephone. Grandmother Gould told my mother, "Ken is a good boy!" She was forceful in saying, "He goes to work and school and does not get in trouble with the law. You need to stop your foolishness and leave that boy alone!"

Grandmother Gould then said, "By the way, this is my house, which I inherited from my older sister. If anybody gets put out of this house, it will be your daddy! He is out right now with one of his sluts!" It was great to hear my grandmother standing up to my mother for me. My mother then told my grandmother, "I called Ken's girlfriend's house and talked to her mother about him. I told his girlfriend's mother that Ken is disrespectful and he caused me to have a nervous breakdown." My grandmother was shocked to hear that. "I also told her to stop Ken from coming to her house. I got their telephone number from John. He knew Terri's mother. John went to school with me in Mount Gilead and now lives in Newport News." My grandmother said, "I don't care! Leave that boy alone." She hung up the telephone while my mother was still talking.

The next evening, Grandfather Gould said, "Grandboy, I apologize for threatening to put you out of the house." He then said, "I don't know what's wrong with your mother. She has had a mental condition for years, even before you were born. When she was young, she claimed someone used witchcraft and caused her to have a nervous breakdown. After you were born, she blamed you for her nervous breakdown. Your grandmother and I and your father tried to take her to a doctor, but she always refused. She accused us of trying to hurt her."

TERRI'S MISCARRIAGE

Although Terri was pregnant and we were engaged, Terri had

serious concerns about meeting her future mother-in-law. I tried to allay her fears by telling her that we were surrounded by family love in Newport News and that should be her primary focus. Plus, my leaving in a few months to go on active duty in the army in April 1968 put a lot of stress on Terri.

Early one morning, I received a telephone call from Mrs. Jason. She said Terri had a miscarriage and was taken to the hospital by ambulance. She advised me that she would stay with Terri all day and I should come by the hospital to see her after I got off work.

That afternoon, when I arrived at the hospital with flowers for Terri, tears started flowing down her face. I asked, "Are you okay?" She said, "I'm sorry for losing our baby." I just held her in my arms and tried to comfort her.

A few days later, we caught a taxicab from the hospital to her mother's house. Mrs. Jason was waiting for us in the living room. In a very calm voice, she said, "Now I understand why you and Terri wanted to get married so soon." Her mother then said, "I noticed Terri was gaining weight. I thought it was from eating too much!"

Later that week, Mrs. Jason gave me the hospital bill, and I paid the bill in installments.

CHRISTMAS 1967

I decided to stay in Newport News with Terri for Christmas. After she recovered from the miscarriage, we had a joyous Christmas celebration, eating good food, exchanging gifts with her family, and going to house parties.

I was soon scheduled to go on active duty with the US Army, so I wanted the remaining time to be happy with Terri. In January 1968, although my money was tight from sending my $500 to North Carolina to my mother and paying the hospital bill, we pooled our money to buy her a used gray Mustang. She was so proud and happy to buy her first car. I wanted her to be independent while I was away in the army and not depend on other people or city buses for transportation.

LEAVING MY JOB IN THE SHIPYARD

In March 1968, I told my supervisor that I would like to take thirty days off work before going on active duty. He granted permission and told me I would receive my next paycheck in two weeks in the mail. This paycheck would also include accrued vacation time. That was music to my ears. He also said, "Because you're a hard worker, when you return from the military, I want you to rejoin my work crew." He shook my hand and wished me well.

On April 4, 1968, four days before I reported to military duty, Dr. Martin Luther King Jr. was murdered. A few young blacks protested his murder by looting and burning down stores. The Newport News black community became a towering inferno. Stores and other buildings burned for several days.

There was another issue that fueled black citizens' frustration: white policemen constantly harassed black people. They arbitrarily harassed and bullied black citizens. For example, one Saturday afternoon, I was walking on Jefferson Avenue when I saw two white policemen driving slowly in their car. A young black man with a visible serious mental health condition was walking ahead of me. He was obviously afraid of policemen and decided to run. When a policeman saw him running, he jumped out of the car and chased him. Eventually, the young man stopped and sat down on the sidewalk.

The angry police officer approached him, pulled out his black nightstick, and was getting ready to hit the young man. A large group of black citizens surrounded the white officer and demanded that he leave the young man alone. Some black males shouted, "If you hit him, we are going to hit you! You see the young man has a mental problem." The officer became very nervous and red-faced and did not hit the young man. His partner never got out of the police car. The black citizens then talked about how white policemen constantly harassed this young man just for fun. It was rumored the then Newport News police chief was a card-carrying member of the Ku Klux Klan.

CHAPTER 33

REPORTING FOR ACTIVE DUTY IN THE US ARMY

Early morning on April 8, 1968, was finally here. After the bus departed Newport News, I fell asleep and woke up at the military induction station in Raleigh, North Carolina. That afternoon, all recruits were transported to a nearby hotel for the night. Two recruits were assigned to each hotel room.

Early the next morning, after breakfast, we reported to the military induction center. We were given numerous physicals and mental tests. Later, military staff announced names of recruits who were going to basic military training to either Fort Bragg, North Carolina, for the army or Parris Island, South Carolina, for the marines. I was told to get in line with army recruits. Up to this point, military staff seemed to be very cordial. I began to wonder if the horror stories about the army were true. We had an enjoyable bus ride to the army base in Fort Bragg, North Carolina.

ARRIVING FOR BASIC TRAINING AT FORT BRAGG, NORTH CAROLINA

The courteous behavior from military personnel was over. When army drill sergeants entered the bus, wearing Smokey Bear's hats, all hell broke loose. They cursed, shouted, and made us move quickly to get off the bus. Drill sergeants got so close to our faces, shouting, until the brim of their Smokey Bear hats touched our foreheads.

Most of the drill sergeants were airborne soldiers and had served in infantry units in Vietnam. My first impression of these drill sergeants was, these men were crazy. Suddenly, all of us army recruits had the same name: maggot.

The next eight weeks of basic training were grueling, both physically and mentally. Thanks to my mother's abuse, I had developed mental toughness and was able to handle the drill sergeants' insulting behavior. Thanks to my father, Grandfather Little, and Grandfather Gould teaching me to be a man from the age of eight through nineteen, I conquered the army's physical activities. On the final physical training test, I scored 497 out of a possible 500 points. I stumbled on the last lap of the one-mile-run test and lost three points. I was proud of my results and was ready to be a good soldier like my father.

After the final physical training test, it was very rewarding for drill sergeants to no longer refer to us as maggots but soldiers in the US Army.

I would be remiss if I didn't thank Grandmother Little and Grandmother Gould for their loving support. Their love gave me a sense of purpose.

Growing up, I recalled hearing the adage "What doesn't kill you makes you stronger." God brought me out of the valley and onto the mountaintop once again. I survived the rigorous basic training at Fort Bragg, and this accomplishment gave my self-esteem a big boost.

I called Terri to tell her about experiences in my basic training and to share my graduation date. She promised to drive down to Fort Bragg, North Carolina, for the graduation ceremony. But she did not show up for the ceremony, and I was so disappointed.

My parents drove down to Fort Bragg but were too late for the ceremony, as I had already departed on a military bus going to Fort Dix, New Jersey. Later that evening, I arrived at Fort Dix for my clerical school training.

After two weeks of training, I was given a three-day pass. I caught a taxicab to the airport and purchased a round-trip ticket from Fort Dix, New Jersey, to Newport News, Virginia. At this point, Terri had stopped sending letters to me.

RUNNING TOWARD ANGER AND HEARTACHE

After the airplane landed in Newport News, I walked outside the airport to a major highway to thumb a ride. Recognizing that I was in a military uniform, a military officer stopped and gave me a ride to the Newport News city limits. Being physically fit, I decided to run down Jefferson Avenue toward Terri's new apartment. As I was running, I saw Terri driving by in her gray Mustang—the car I helped her purchase.

I yelled, "Terri!" She stopped abruptly, and I ran over to the car and started kissing her. She seemed non-responsive and had a frightened look on her face. Right then, I looked up and saw a man sitting in the passenger seat. We stared at each other for a few minutes. I backed away from the car, as I was full of anger and heartache. She finally said, "I will be right back," and drove off.

Apparently, she drove somewhere and dropped the man off.

I walked toward my grandparents' house. It appeared that Terri drove around until she found me. She drove up beside me and said, "Please get into the car, Kenny."

I said to her, "You are being unfaithful, and I have been away in the army for only ten weeks! Looks like I loved you more, Terri, than you loved me. Before I left, I thought we had a strong bond and were on our way to getting married soon."

I suddenly had a flashback. I remembered how she dropped her former marine boyfriend while he was on active duty. Fast-forward, she dropped me after I joined the army. In hindsight, maybe I should have been patient and devoted my time to Mandy.

After taking my engagement ring from Terri, I rode the city bus uptown and pawned the rings. The rings had a store value of $250. Without love, the rings had lost their shine and had no value to me. I pawned the rings for $50. I wanted to bring closure to this CHAPTER of my life.

GRANDMOTHER GOULD'S WISDOM

I spent most of the day talking to Grandmother Gould. As usual, Grandfather Gould was not at home; he was out chasing women.

Toward the end of the day, Grandmother Gould asked me, "Why do you look so unhappy? You are not yourself! Are you having girlfriend problems?" Then she jokingly said, "You know, when the cat's away, the rat will play!" Lastly, my grandmother said, "Dealing with heartbreak is a part of life. Just don't get stuck there! Grandboy, move on with your life. When one door closes, a better one opens!"

I think Grandmother Gould knew something about Terri. I am guessing Terri's cousin Marilyn called Mandy at college in North Carolina and told her about Terri's new man. In turn, Mandy called

Grandmother Gould and told her about Terri's new affair. Bad news travels fast.

LOVE THIEF

From personal experience, I need to talk about the "love thief." The love thief's goal is to steal lovers' happiness and drive a wedge between them. Initially, when lovers first experience a long-distance relationship, they make strong commitments to each other within their minds and hearts. The love thief waits patiently in dark shadows for one or both lovers to become weak. As time goes by, the mind loses its focus and the heart grows lonely. The patient love thief then pounces on its prey—a lonely man or woman. The love thief will steal your lover and give your lover to another.

The love thief knows that lovers are accustomed to having constant intimate affairs with each other. Oftentimes, lovers have no intentions of betraying each other. But after a long time and long distance, lovers slowly submit to seductive temptation. The love thief uses seductive temptation to expose one or both lovers to a new person. Eventually, seductive temptation overpowers a man or woman, and they submit to a new person's lust and companionship.

It takes exceptional lovers with deep-rooted love and commitment to each other to withstand the love thief's evil deception. Please do not let the love thief betray you or your lover by dangling a new person in your face.

You must ignore the love thief's deceitful tactics. Whether your lover is near or far, please try to fall in love with each other every day. If not, please remember the love thief will steal your lover and give your lover to another.

CHAPTER 34

REFLECTIONS ON MY LIFE

AIRPLANE FLIGHT BACK
TO FORT DIX, NEW JERSEY

When I boarded the airplane, I reflected on my life in Newport News. I was romantically involved with two or more women and woke up each day with a smile on my face. Now I did not have a lover to call my own. Mandy was away at college, pursuing a college degree and having fun, and Terri had a new man. The adage "Every dog has his day" resonated in my mind. I guess the label Mandy gave me was true; I was a dog like Grandfather Gould.

I also reflected on my formative years as a teenager. I remembered an older lady in Badin, North Carolina, named Helen telling me a short story about a dog. I guess she saw my potential of becoming a dog at a young age. The potential of being a dog was in my bloodline, just like Mother and Grandfather Gould.

The lady told me, one day, a dog was walking by a river with a bone in his mouth. The dog looked down into the water and saw what he thought was another dog with a bone in his mouth. The dog pondered for a second and decided to steal the other dog's bone so he would have two bones. The dog opened his mouth to take the other dog's bone and dropped his bone in the river. In doing so, the dog lost his bone and ended up with nothing.

That day, I felt like that dog—I lost both lovers. I had no one to love or to love me. I then wondered if the last two years of my life were real or just an illusion. Regardless, it was fun while it lasted.

GRADUATING FROM FORT DIX'S CLERICAL SCHOOL

When the eight weeks of clerical training was over, I passed my final clerical test and graduated. One day, while we were standing in military formation, the company's first sergeant (E-8) passed out individual military orders for new military base assignments. I was ordered to take thirty days' military leave (vacation) and then report back to Fort Dix for a military flight to Frankfurt, Germany. My new duty station was in Karlsruhe, Germany.

I decided to fly from Fort Dix, New Jersey, to Charlotte, North Carolina, the nearest airport to my house. It was forty-two miles from my house in New London, North Carolina. My father picked me up at the airport. I spent my entire thirty days on military leave in New London.

One exception: I drove to Mount Gilead, North Carolina, several times to visit Grandfather and Grandmother Little and Aunt Ellen. We laughed, talked, and ate delicious food. I told them my next military duty assignment was in Germany and not Vietnam. They were happy.

Grandmother Little told me that having three sons fighting in Germany during World War II was nerve-racking for the family. She was thankful that God allowed her sons to make it back home alive. She then told me, "You be a good boy while stationed in Germany. Don't get in trouble over there." I promised to be a good boy.

CHAPTER 35

MY MOTHER'S DIRTY THREAT TO GET A MONTHLY MILITARY ALLOTMENT

When I was at home, my mother badgered me daily about sending her a monthly military allotment when I arrived in Germany. She said, "You don't need money in Germany because the army feeds you three meals a day. Your rent is free, and your military uniforms are free."

I told her the army pays me $97.50 per month. She got angry and said, "I can always write a letter to your new company commander and tell him your family is experiencing hardship and we need your monthly wages at home." She learned these dirty games while my father was in the army during World War II. I am sure my father coached my mother on this dirty scheme. He did it to impress her with his knowledge of the military. He probably shared stories of how black soldiers in his unit experienced a family member writing a hardship letter to the company commander to get a portion of his monthly wages.

I knew my new company commander in Germany would not send my entire $97.50 to my mother each month based on her bullcrap. To avoid an embarrassing situation between my mother and my new company commander in Germany, I agreed to send her $20 each month. For the remaining of my thirty days' leave, I avoided my mother.

On my last day at home, a former classmate named Jerry drove me to Charlotte to catch my flight to Fort Dix, New Jersey, because my father was working. He was on active duty in the army and had military orders to report to Vietnam and join an infantry unit. I offered to pay him for the ride, but he refused. I wished him a safe journey, and we went our separate ways.

REPORTING FOR MILITARY DUTY

I reported back to Fort Dix on a Sunday and had a few days' layover on base. Then one evening, a group of us were shipped over to McGuire Air Force Base to catch an airplane bound for Frankfurt, Germany. We left late that evening and arrived in Frankfurt early the next morning.

We were met at the airport by a sergeant who was stationed in Karlsruhe. Later, we boarded a commercial German train bound for Karlsruhe. While riding the train, soldiers whispered to each other about feeling uncomfortable because German citizens stared at us. Several hours later, we arrived at Karlsruhe's commercial train station. An army driver was there waiting and transported us to Karlsruhe's US military base. We were assigned to temporary barracks for several days. I was given a permanent barracks and workplace assignment within a week. I worked with several other clerk typists in an office.

I wrote a letter to my parents letting them know I had arrived safely in Germany. The following week, I received a letter from my mother stating that I owed her $250 for new car tires. She claimed I wore the family's car tires out by driving too much while on thirty days' military leave at home. I never responded.

I arrived in Germany in late summer in 1968. As documented in history books, on the nights of August 20–21, 1968, the Soviet Union (now named Russia) and its main allies in the Warsaw Pact (Bulgaria, Hungry, East Germany, and Poland) invaded the Czechoslovak Socialist Republic. Approximately 500,000 troops attacked and killed 108 civilians and wounded 500 more. This attack was done to halt political liberalism reforms in Czechoslovakia. Our US base in Karlsruhe, Germany, was put on full combat alert with anticipation of going to war with the Soviet Union and its allies. Every US soldier was issued combat gear, M16 rifles, and ammunition and was restricted to base. This was a very scary moment for us; fortunately, we were never called into military action.

That incident haunted me. For months, I stayed in seclusion on base. I never went off base to explore the city of Karlsruhe. I think it was because I was unsure if war was pending. I developed a pattern of going to the mess hall to eat, going to work, and going to the military base club to drink a beer. Sometimes I played two songs repeatedly on the jukebox in the club, "What Becomes of the Broken Hearted" by the late Jimmy Ruffin and "Love Is a Hurtin' Thing" by the late Lou Rawls. It took a while, but I eventually recovered from the heartbreak.

I also enjoyed going to the military base club when German bands performed for us. The fascinating part of their performance was, they could sing American songs in English but they could not speak fluent English.

Eventually, I decided to venture out in downtown Karlsruhe. Although it was in the late 1960s, some German citizens still harbored racist attitudes toward Americans, especially black soldiers. Racism was perpetuated by Germany's late Nazi leader, Adolf Hitler. He left a large racist footprint on Germany.

The racist attitude was a carryover from losing World War II. Some Germans were still angry about losing World War II to the United States and its allies in 1945. According to history books, Adolf Hitler murdered more than six million people during his reign as Führer in Germany. Rather than facing penalties for his heinous crimes, he committed a cowardly act: he chose to commit suicide. Hitler supposedly died from a self-inflicted gunshot wound to the head.

German citizens' anger was focused on mostly black soldiers. When we went downtown and attempted to enter selected nightclubs, German employees showed us a sign with big bold letters with the inscription, "off limits to US soldiers". Coincidently, black soldiers recognized white soldiers assigned to our army base drinking and having fun in some "off limits" nightclubs. The German employees knew they were white soldiers because they could not speak the German language.

One bad situation demonstrated the extremely high racial climate on the US Army base in Karlsruhe in 1968. A white soldier supposedly single-handedly killed three black soldiers in a downtown German nightclub. He was later found not guilty by a panel of white US military officers. After the "not guilty" verdict for the white soldier became public, the base commander ordered all soldiers on lockdown in their barracks.

To maintain peace or avoid unrest, white military officers rushed to transfer that white soldier out of Germany. He was sent to an unknown location.

I knew it was time for me to leave Germany. I then decided to focus on how to better myself. I explored the possibility of volunteering for duty in Vietnam. I discussed my idea with an enlisted (E) career soldier named Staff Sergeant Stewart (E-6), who had served in Vietnam. His first comment was "Vietnam is very dangerous, and you are committed to serving twelve months in country."

He then pointed out five benefits of serving in Vietnam: (1) military pay in Vietnam is tax free; (2) the army offered and I should take advantage of the 10 percent interest soldier's saving plan; (3) the army offered each soldiers seven days of rest and recuperation (R&R) in countries in close proximity to Vietnam; (4) military rank is earned faster in Vietnam, and since I was already a specialist fourth class (E-4), I should get promoted to specialist fifth class (E-5) in no time; and (5) with a transfer to Vietnam, I would get free thirty days leave in the United States before reporting to Vietnam.

My primary focus was on one statement the staff sergeant made: I would get free thirty days leave in the United States before reporting to Vietnam.

CHAPTER 36

RECEIVED MILITARY ORDERS FOR REASSIGNMENT IN VIETNAM

I served seven months in Germany and finally received military orders for reassignment in Saigon, Vietnam. I was granted thirty days' leave. It was mid-April 1969 when I flew out of Frankfurt, Germany, and landed at Fort Dix, New Jersey. After a short layover, I flew from New Jersey to Patrick Henry Airport in Newport News, Virginia.

VISITING GRANDFATHER AND GRANDMOTHER GOULD

When I arrived, Grandmother Gould was at home and told me she was so glad to see me. As usual, Grandfather Gould was not at home. I telephoned a food order into a delivery café. When the food arrived, we sat down, ate dinner, and talked about my army life for most of the evening.

I went to bed early that night as I was exhausted from the airplane flights from Germany to New Jersey and from New Jersey to Newport News, Virginia. Grandfather Gould came home later that night and knocked on my bedroom door to wake me up. I got out of bed and talked to him for hours about my army experiences. The next morning, I got up and ate breakfast with my grandparents. I later caught a taxicab to the bus station, bought a bus ticket, and traveled to Albemarle, North Carolina. I arrived at my parents' house in New London, North Carolina, late that evening.

MY MOTHER'S CONTINUOUS GREED FOR MONEY

My parents told me I could use the family car for the remainder of my military leave. Before I left the house, my mother told me, "I want you to send me more than $20 each month." To prevent her from taking the car from me, I promised to increase the dollar amount. That made her happy.

TALKING TO MY GREEN TREE LEAVES

Early the next day, while the wet morning dew was still on the green tree leaves, I climbed the tall tree near the house. I told the green tree leaves that I was happy to be back in the United States and I would be home for twenty-seven more days of military leave. I advised them that my next military assignment was in Saigon, Vietnam. They gasped and said they would be praying for me while stationed in Vietnam. They knew I would return home safe. I thanked them for their vote of confidence.

VISITING GRANDFATHER AND GRANDMOTHER LITTLE AND AUNT ELLEN

After the green tree leaves and I finished our group hug, I drove to Mount Gilead, North Carolina, to see Grandfather and Grandmother Little and Aunt Ellen. On the way to their house, I stopped and bought a six-pack of beer. When Grandmother Little saw me open a can of beer, she exploded with anger. She said, "Boy, what are you doing drinking alcohol?" She then pointed her finger at me and said, "When you were a young boy, you cried and told me,'I will never drink alcohol because it makes my mother and father argue and fight.'"

I dropped my head in shame and told Grandmother Little, "I am sorry, and you are the last person on earth whom I would tell a deliberate lie!" Displaying emotion, I said to my grandmother, "I lost a young lady I loved very much while away in the army. I just need a beer to relax my nerves."

She said, "Come here, boy, and give me a big hug." After she finished hugging me, she said, "Do you remember when you were a little boy, sitting beside me in church, and I started crying out of control?" I motioned "Yes" with my head. "I remember saying to you that you would understand one day! Today is just one of the many challenges in life you will experience. You, too, will cry out loud in church one day. Boy, do not stay stuck in sadness. Reach your hand and heart out to God for guidance and support. Listen carefully, and believe me, I know the best is yet to come in your life. Keep marching forward, soldier!" Grandmother Little went on to say, "Your grandfather and father raised you to be a hardworking, responsible man. Responsible young ladies look for these traits in a future husband. You're a young man—get out there, have some fun, and enjoy life!" As tears flowed down my face, I gave Grandmother

Little another big hug.

By the time I was ready to leave, Grandfather Little had grabbed the remaining five beers, rolled them in newspaper, and retreated to the outdoor toilet to drink them. The superintendent of the church, who abstained from drinking alcohol, was in rare form when he returned to the house. He was laughing and telling jokes. That was Grandfather Little!

While I was talking to my grandparents, Aunt Ellen prepared dinner. I changed my mind about leaving right then. I sat down at the table, tasted the food, and reminisced about how much I enjoyed her cooking as a young boy. I could still taste the love in the food she cooked. After I stuffed myself, I felt like going to sleep. Instead, I drove from Mount Gilead to Badin, North Carolina, looking for any young lady to take out on a date. I was on the prowl for a short-term romance.

LOOKING FOR ROMANCE

When I arrived in Badin, I went into a bootlegger's club located in an isolated area in the woods. The club had one way in and one way out. I bought a beer, placed my back against the wall, and checked out the flow of young ladies coming into the club. I wanted to avoid asking a married or a single lady who was in a committed relationship for a date. I was there looking for fun and romance and not a fight. After a while, I made eye contact with an attractive young lady at the far side of the club.

I walked across the club, introduced myself, and engaged her in a conversation. She told me her name was Tammy. Surprisingly, she said, "Do you remember me? I rode your school bus to North Stanly High School! I graduated from high school last year." I lied and said, "Yes, I remember you. I never forget a pretty face!" Tammy stood there blushing while I was doing the math in my head and concluded she was over eighteen years old and legal to date. My twenty-first birthday was just months away, in the summer of 1969. Someone played a slow song on the jukebox and I said, "Tammy, do you think your boyfriend would mind if you slow danced with me?" She replied, "He was drafted into the army and left for Fort Bragg, North Carolina, last week."

One part of her statement made me feel sad, as I was in Fort Bragg when Terri betrayed me. The other part of her statement about her boyfriend being in the army was music to my ears.

I then decided to test her loyalty to her boyfriend. I pulled her close while we slow danced and started bumping and grinding. If she backed away, I would apologize and pretend to be a gentleman. Fortunately for me, she held me tight and gave new meaning to bumping and grinding. It felt like we were having sex with our clothes on!

After the dance, we went into a dimly lit room. We ordered two fried chicken sandwiches drenched in hot sauce and wrapped in wax paper. We also ordered two sixteen-ounce cans of beer, and she requested a $1 shot of brown liquor (bourbon). After we finished our food and drinks, Tammy said, "Let's go for a ride to see what's happening at the bootlegger's club in Albemarle, North Carolina." Strange enough, the club was closed.

While driving back toward Badin, I suggested that we drive to Badin Lake, park, and walk along the water. In the late 1960s, Badin Lake was segregated. Black people had to drive on a dirt road deep into the woods to have access to the lake. White people accessed the lake from the main highway that had a paved U-shaped parking lot.

It was a windy night, and the mist from the water put a chill in the air. Tammy said, "I'm cold. Let's go back and sit in the car." As we approached the car, I opened the door to the back seat. Without hesitation, Tammy climbed into the back seat. I went into my wallet and pulled out protection. She immediately started to undress. When the fun was over, I drove her home. I spent the next three weeks dating Tammy.

After I made love to Tammy one night, I thought to myself that the late 1960s was a peace movement era. The movement evolved with youth protesting US military personnel fighting in the Vietnam conflict. Vietnam is located approximately ten thousand miles away from the United States. While protesting the conflict, youth often shouted the slogan "Make Love, Not War!" Along with shouting the slogan, they freely participated in making love. I did not protest, but I participated in making love.

Information circulated that Tammy later moved out of state, became an escort, and was brutally murdered because of her lifestyle. I was shocked and upset to hear this information.

BUS RIDE FROM SALISBURY, NORTH CAROLINA

When my military leave was over in May 1969, my father drove twenty-three miles to Salisbury, North Carolina, so I could catch the bus back to Fort Dix, New Jersey. We barely said a word to each other during the drive. When we arrived at the bus station, surprisingly, he parked the car and came inside. He walked halfway through the station, stopped, and looked at me and said, "Boy, when you arrive in Vietnam, follow the sergeant's orders, and you will come back home alive." I reached out to shake his hand, but he turned around, walked toward the bus station door, and never looked back. I wondered if he was crying because I was going to Vietnam. I stood there a few minutes and wondered why he just walked away. I watched him until he exited the bus station. This was a tender moment for both of us.

Shortly after I boarded the bus in Salisbury, I had a brief

layover in Greensboro, North Carolina. The bus was full of passengers. As we were leaving Greensboro, I was nodding off to sleep. Suddenly, a white state patrolman stopped the bus and asked the bus driver if there were any young colored boys on the bus. The bus driver replied, "Yes. He is wearing a military uniform." The patrolman stepped onto the bus, pointed at me, and told me to get off the bus. I complied.

Just to demonstrate to the patrolman that he was dealing with a soldier, when I got off the bus, I assumed the military stance of "Attention." I placed my cuffed fingers on both sides of my pants, thumbs touching the outer seams of my pants, heels locked, and shoes pointed at a forty-five-degree angle. I stared directly into the patrolman's eyes. The patrolman and I played the racist staring game for a few minutes. Racists hate it when as strong black man stares into their eyes. They try to use the staring game to intimidate black people.

The patrolman then asked if I had been on A&T State University's campus (historically black university) that day. With a puzzled look on my face, I responded no. I told him I got on the bus in Salisbury and I was on my way to Vietnam. He asked the bus driver, "Did this boy get on the bus in Salisbury?" The bus driver replied yes. As I evaluated the patrolman's body language, I could tell he was feeling really stupid. He then said, "Okay, get back on the bus, boy!" I also sensed he did not have good intentions when he asked me to get off the bus. I know my military uniform saved my life.

As I walked toward my seat on the bus, black and white people apologized to me for being harassed by the patrolman. One lady shouted out that he had no right to harass a US soldier. I thanked them.

I later found out that North Carolina's Army National Guard had been in a shootout with black student protesters at North

Carolina A&T State University.

A few days later, I flew from Fort Dix, New Jersey, to Seattle, Washington for a one-week jungle warfare training.

REPORTING FOR MILITARY DUTY

Seattle, Washington, had a very rainy environment, like weather conditions in Vietnam. Soldiers in my group had military orders for Vietnam. We were issued M16 rifles, special, lightweight green jungle fatigues (daily military uniform in Vietnam), green underwear, and lightweight black-and-green jungle combat boots.

Jungle training was very intense and raised soldiers' stress levels in the simulated jungle environment. There were numerous hidden empty land mines, camouflaged deep holes in the ground with sharp wooden spikes, trip wires for explosives, surprise enemy ambushes, and others. This training made us realize that we had to be extremely alert to survive in Vietnam.

After completing the training, we were transported by bus to military barracks (living quarters) on Edwards Air Force Base (AFB) in California. Air force mattresses on bunk beds were significantly thicker than the army's thin mattresses. Mess hall (eating area) food was delicious. Air force personnel lived a comfortable lifestyle. Two days later, we boarded an airplane at Edwards AFB bound for South Vietnam.

CHAPTER 37

AIRPLANE FLIGHT TO SOUTH VIETNAM

It was a grueling twenty-one-hour flight from California to South Vietnam, and we made several airplane refueling stops along the way; however, soldiers were not allowed to get off the airplane. We were stuffed into tight seats, and after a while, airplane air ventilations circulated soldiers' bad body odor. On a positive note, soldiers were laughing, talking loudly, and listening to music. Flight attendants frequently served us snacks, hot meals, and beverages.

As the airplane descended from the air into South Vietnam, the soldiers' noise levels decreased. When we landed and flight attendants opened the airplane doors, soldiers were silently praying. I bowed my head and said a silent prayer as well.

WELCOME TO VIETNAM, OR "THE BUSH"

Because of thick jungle vegetation, combat soldiers nicknamed Vietnam the Bush. My tour of duty in Vietnam started in May 1969 and was scheduled to end in May 1970. As I exited the airplane, I felt the extremely hot air and humidity, and the temperature was over one hundred degrees. Sweat immediately saturated my face, body, and jungle fatigues (uniform). The smell of death lingered in the air; it reeked the horrible smell of burned human flesh. Heavy smog cluttered my eyes and affected my breathing. My body and stomach were trembling, and I was extremely nervous.

I heard loud American B-52 bomber jets constantly taking off and landing at the military air base. Off in the distance, I heard bomber jets dropping bombs. This caused the ground to vibrate under my feet. Numerous American helicopters sprinkled the sky. Door gunners (soldiers) were hanging outside helicopter doors. They were armed with powerful long-barrel machine guns that dangled in the air outside helicopter doors. Vietnam was a helicopter conflict! They were used daily to transport soldiers to and from the jungle to fight enemy soldiers and transport wounded and deceased soldiers from the jungle. They were also used to transport food, weapons, ammunition, and other supplies.

Decades later, that distinct sound of helicopter propellers flying overhead continues to echo in my head. Although I am in the United States, I still tend to look toward the sky when a helicopter flies over-head. The loud helicopter sound creates anxiety and flashbacks to Vietnam for me.

Back to my first day in Vietnam, I saw numerous combat soldiers walking around with stressful looks on their faces. They wore dirty, faded, weather-beaten military jungle fatigues with red mud covering their combat boots.

As a shock factor, one infantry soldier walked over to us to show his homemade necklace. It was a thick white string that dangled around his neck. It showed one ear of each enemy soldier he had killed in combat. He laughed as we quickly walked away from him. Several of these soldiers looked at us new soldiers in country wearing clean jungle fatigues and spit-shined boots and shouted, "Short!" This was a popular slogan among soldiers who were within days of completing a mandatory twelve-month tour in South Vietnam. They were happy to endure the grueling twenty-one-hour airplane flight back to the "world" (USA).

After I secured my duffel bag, I was put in military formation with other soldiers. When my name was called, I fell out of military formation and reported to my group leader. I then boarded a military bus equipped with heavy metal screens on the windows. The metal screens prevented Vietcong (enemy soldiers or civilians) from throwing deadly hand grenades (explosive devices) on the bus. After what seemed like an hour's drive, I arrived at the military personnel office at my new duty station in Saigon, Vietnam.

I filled out military forms and noted my beneficiaries (my father and mother) for a $10,000 life insurance policy. I sent a copy of the insurance policy to my parents in New London, North Carolina. I also joined a 10 percent interest soldier's savings plan. Military finance personnel deducted 10 percent of my tax-free monthly pay and deposited this money into my savings plan. Soldiers were prohibited from withdrawing money from this plan until permanently returning to the United States. I now had attained the enlisted rank of specialist fourth class (E-4). My tax-free salary allowed me to make a decent monthly deposit into my plan.

My next stop was the military supply office. I was issued additional pairs of green jungle fatigues and green underwear. I was also issued a brand-new M16 rifle and ammunition.

Lastly, I was given written orders (paperwork) on where to report for work the next day. The personnel clerk told me, "Your job is in an office responsible for receiving and processing the army's highly classified (intelligence) materials."

I grabbed my duffel bag and reported to First Sergeant Johnson (E-8), responsible for the newly built two-story barracks. The first sergeant assigned me to a bay (living area) with a bunk bed, a tall gray wall locker, and a green wooden footlocker. Bunk beds were stacked high to provide sleeping arrangements for two soldiers. Latrines (bathrooms) were large enough to accommodate numerous soldiers. The barracks seemed to cover an area like five city blocks. At least thirty soldiers lived in each barrack's bay, on both sides of the building.

There was one unexpected luxury. I was surprised to find in the US Army, soldiers were assigned Vietnamese maid service in the barracks. The maids washed, starched, and ironed military uniforms; spit-shined jungle boots, washed and changed bunk bed linen, cleaned latrines, and mopped and cleaned the barrack's general living areas. Soldiers stationed at US military bases performed these duties.

I paid my maid a monthly salary. If a soldier failed to pay his maid, this resulted in disciplinary action by the barrack's First Sergeant Johnson. This action included a pay reduction or working in the mess hall kitchen (kitchen patrol or KP) for an extended period.

A few soldiers were insensitive and openly expressed their hatred for all Vietnamese. They often referred to Vietnamese using racist labels. I concluded that these soldiers also used racist labels to identify black and other ethnic American soldiers. Most racist soldiers were easy to identify, as they had Confederate flags mounted on barracks walls near their bunks. The Confederate flags did not intimidate black soldiers. Our position was, "If you don't bother me, I will not bother you." The Confederate flag owners usually isolated themselves from most soldiers.

My maid introduced herself to me and said, "My name Huang." She then told me that she was going to have a baby in one month and would return to work for me. Her husband was a South Vietnamese soldier fighting Vietcong (enemy soldiers). My first and lasting impression of Huang was that she was a very nice lady.

During my tour in Vietnam, Huang's husband was killed in combat. She was so sad and grief-stricken. Grandmother Little always told me, "Treat people nice, and the Lord will bless you." Her words motivated me to give Huang extra money each month to help support her three children.

REPORTING TO MY NEW DUTY ASSIGNMENT

Early the next morning, after eating breakfast in the mess hall, I reported to my new duty assignment, the message center. Initially, I met with Colonel Watson and Master Sergeant Gibbs (E-8). They oversaw the message center and the mail room. I was then taken to my new work area and introduced to the staff of military officers and enlisted men.

My immediate supervisor was Sergeant First Class Winston (E-7), a career white soldier with a close crew cut hairstyle from Alabama. My first thought was, I have a racist supervisor. He was short in stature and had a mean demeanor.

He explained the office operations to me and added that we have another office down the hall responsible for making two daily mail courier runs to deliver classified materials to the American Embassy in Saigon. Other deliveries were made to United States and South Vietnamese military bases outside Saigon. He also told me, in addition to processing classified material, they processed fast-moving B-52 jet bombing requests to support US combat infantry units under fire in the jungle. Sometimes helicopter units were also sent into the jungle to provide air combat support for US infantry units.

The office was open twenty-four hours a day, seven days a week. Three teams of soldiers worked 10-hour shifts and rotated shifts every 30 days. It did not take long for me to adjust to working

10-hour shifts. Starting at age 8, Grandfather Little had groomed me to work long hours in cotton fields in Mount Gilead, North Carolina. Thank you Grandfather Little!

My first job assignment required me to make numerous copies of classified materials, collate and staple them, and place them in outgoing classified mailboxes. Military officers were required to sign a form when picking up classified materials.

After I had worked in the message center for a month, my first suspicion about Sergeant Winston was confirmed. He did not want me to talk to another black soldier on staff named Jasper. White soldiers talked freely and joked openly at work.

Eventually, I was transferred to another team in the message center. My new supervisor's name was Sergeant First Class Martinez (E-7). I observed that he was observing my work habits very closely. After two months went by, one afternoon, he called me into the office and said, "Sergeant Winston [Alabama racist] told me that you were lazy and that was why you were transferred to my team. I have watched you closely for the past two months and concluded that you have excellent work habits."

He then added, "To be open with you, Little, Sergeant Winston does not like black or Hispanic soldiers." Sergeant Martinez shook my hand and welcomed me to the team.

MY FIRST TWO MONTHS IN VIETNAM

During my first two months in Vietnam, I stayed on base. I felt somewhat secure on base as the commanding general lived in his private trailer just two blocks from the barracks.

Eventually, that secure feeling I initially felt was shaken. Late one night, enemy soldiers sneaked onto our military base and blew up our reserve ammunitions depot. These ammunitions were stored in a building near the general's trailer. That night, we thought the military base was under attack by the enemy. Every soldier in the barracks retrieved ammunition and loaded their M16 rifles. We looked out windows and ran around the barracks in our green army underwear, looking for enemy soldiers.

The US military police made us stand down as the enemy had escaped. How? I later found out enemy soldiers had dug underground tunnels underneath our military base. These tunnels made it easy for them to gain access and exit our military base.

As time passed, I still did not feel secure enough to go to Downtown Saigon to chase ladies and drink beer at different bars. Although for different reasons, I eventually fell into the same rut I was in while stationed in Germany. My daily routine included going to the mess hall to eat, going to work in the message center, drinking beer and listening to music in the enlisted club. I also wrote letters to different people back in the United States and soldiers (homeboys from Badin, North Carolina) stationed in Vietnam. I was in a rut because I missed the familiar—home.

Some nights I would stare out the barrack's window, watching US jets drop bombs on the enemy near Saigon. The dark horizons turned bright red after bombs exploded. Jungle vegetation burned with bright-red flames. The bombs caused our barrack's windows to shake and floors to vibrate. The sound of US helicopter propellers flapping in the air was forever present twenty-four hours each day. On one hand, the helicopter sound made me feel safe, but on the other hand, it increased my anxiety. I observed several times helicopters were hovering overhead near our barracks. Suddenly, captured enemy soldiers were being tossed out of helicopters. My first thought was, "Oh, crap!" Seeing atrocities of human bodies being tossed from helicopters is still etched in my mind today.

During the first two months, my life was like the movie Groundhog Day. I experienced the same recurring events each day.

MY FIRST NIGHT IN DOWNTOWN SAIGON

One evening, while I was drinking beer in the enlisted club, my drinking buddies started teasing me about staying on the military base every night. I had five drinking buddies in Vietnam: a career army staff sergeant (E-6) from North Carolina named Rick; a career air force staff sergeant (E-5) from Detroit named Paul; an army draftee specialist fifth class (E-5) from Texas named Chuck; an army draftee specialist fourth class (E-4) from Louisiana named Greg; and an army draftee specialist fourth class (E-4) from Georgia named Bill. Over time, we developed strong camaraderies like blood brothers.

My drinking buddies told me that if I stayed on base any longer, my testicles would swell and explode. After enduring hours of harassment, I caught the military bus with them and went downtown (Saigon). I felt so nervous during the bus ride.

When we arrived in Saigon, we danced with young ladies and had fun at the first bar. We then barhopped, drank more beer, and eventually ended up in a "house of ill repute." I instantly connected with a beautiful, dark-skinned Cambodian lady of the evening named Lily. I paid my money, pulled out my wallet, and retrieved my reserve prophylactic. When the fun was over, I started singing the Alka-Seltzer commercial. "Plop, plop, fizz, fizz, oh, what a relief it is!" My buddies cracked up, laughing at me. This became my new routine.

As we were walking toward the military bus stop, gunfire erupted. We thought we were being fired at by enemy soldiers. We hit the ground and started low-crawling on our stomachs through the mud and filthy water to avoid being shot. Suddenly, the gunfire stopped and we heard laughter coming from the top of a nearby two-story building.

To our surprise, it was white American military policemen (MPs) shooting at us with an M-50 machine gun. They were falling over laughing at our reaction to the machine gun fire. Once back on base, we reported the situation to a white officer MP (captain) on duty. He promised to fully investigate the matter, so we gave him our names and office telephone numbers to contact us.

The MP captain was laughing when he called to report his findings. He said the MPs who fired at us thought we were a group of deserters from an infantry unit. What a crock of sh——! Deserters in Vietnam always kept low profiles and never walked on main streets in Saigon. Deserters were from all races in Vietnam. These white MPs were probably bored sitting on top of a building, pulling guard duty. Their mission was to protect US military personnel and not shoot at them. This was a case of overt (open) racism by a white military officer and white MPs.

Because this racist behavior was acceptable in Vietnam, it was transferred to the minds of MPs who later became police officers in the United States. Do I need to say more about racial profiling and police brutality?

I need to add this caveat. This is not an indictment of all white MPs who served in Vietnam. Some were there to protect and serve all US soldiers.

CHAPTER 38

DEAR JOHN LETTERS

My initial twelve-month tour of duty in Vietnam went by slowly. Unfortunately, I was not the only soldier who experienced heartache in the military. Each week, numerous soldiers received Dear John letters from their wives or girlfriends. Their letters stated, "I am sorry, but I did not intend for this to happen. I got weak and fell in love with another man." In some cases, it was a soldier's best friend who stole his lover in the United States.

It was a heart-wrenching sight to see a two-hundred-pound soldier crying on another soldier's shoulder. Soldiers never laughed when soldier buddies received Dear John letters, because they could be next. Since we lacked professional training in dealing with soldiers' psychological problems, we developed a buddy support system. We bought cases of beer from the enlisted club and brought them back into the barracks. While drinking and playing music, we gave soldiers a chance to discuss their heartache. It was the group's unwritten rule to never discuss a soldier buddies' heartbreak issues with outsiders.

For example, one of my soldier buddies named Bill made future plans to marry his fiancée, whom he left back in the "world."

Each month he mailed most of his monthly paychecks home to her to deposit in a joint savings account. One evening, we found him sitting on his bunk, crying out of control. He showed us the Dear John letter he received from his former fiancée. He lost his fiancée and his money. He wanted to seek revenge. We formed a circle around him, and each of us told him how we experienced painful heartbreak. We told him the pain would ease as time went by.

Our layman's support system helped us bond through adversity and brought us together as soldier brothers. No soldier was left behind to suffer alone in silence. It appeared that God allowed a few of us to experience heartache so we could be a blessing to other soldiers. However, some soldiers tried to bury their pain with alcohol and illegal drugs. None of us were immune to heartache and pain.

MY LOVE EQUATION

As previously mentioned, my love equation was tested weekly in Vietnam. The equation was "Lovers with a long time apart plus a long distance apart equal zero love" (long time + long distance = zero love). Before separating, initially, both lovers have good intentions, but in time, love just fades away. This love equation may apply to one or both lovers.

MY PROMOTION TO SPECIALIST FIFTH CLASS (E-5)

After I had been in Vietnam for six months, I noticed white soldiers on my team were being promoted from specialist fourth class (E-4) to specialist fifth class (E-5). This rank is like a sergeant (E-5) and exempts soldiers from menial details, such as kitchen patrol (KP) and others.

I decided to ask a soldier who was recently promoted to E-5 to explain the process for getting promoted to E-5. You need one year in grade as an E-4, and if you have some college experience, it increases your chance of getting promoted. I had one year in grade and one year of community college before enlisting in the army. The soldier then said, "One day, Master Sergeant Gibbs (E-8) from the message center called me into his office and told me he had recommended me for promotion to E-5." I thanked the soldier for the advice.

Immediately, I counted up my months in grade as an E-4. My months in grade as an E-4 exceeded one year. I also had one year of business school in Newport News, Virginia. I walked over to Master Sergeant Gibbs's door and knocked and asked, "May I talk to you about being promoted to E-5?"

His first response was "You have only been in Vietnam around six months."

I responded, "I had six months in grade as an E-4 while stationed in Germany, six months while stationed here in Vietnam, and I have one year of business school."

His face turned flaming red. During a long pause, I could see he was trying hard to think of a reason not to recommend me for promotion. His attitude reminded me of when I was aged eight and the cotton field overseer tried to intimidate me when I asked about my pay shortage. Finally, he said, "Let me look at your military file, and I will get back to you."

I smiled and said, "Thank you, Master Sergeant Gibbs!"

The reason I smiled was that I knew he was looking for negative documented disciplinary actions in my military file as a reason to not promote me to E-5. My military file was clean, with no disciplinary action. In Vietnam, a lot of enlisted black soldiers were stuck at grade E-4 and only complained to one another. Not me, I took action.

A week later, Master Sergeant Gibbs called me into his office and said, "I submitted your name to the promotion board for promotion to E-5. Good luck, Specialist Little!" I shook his hand and thanked him.

Two weeks later, I went before the promotion board and passed. In the ensuing two weeks thereafter, I was promoted to specialist fifth class (E-5). It was a great feeling standing before my office teammates, getting my E-5 pins attached to my collar by Colonel Watson.

In Vietnam, soldiers did not have bright-yellow rank displayed on their sleeves, as in the United States and other countries. In Vietnam, the bright-yellow ranks on soldiers' sleeves made them stand out and made them easy targets for enemy soldiers.

SENDING A LETTER HOME ABOUT MY PROMOTION

I sent a letter home to New London to share the good news about my promotion. Being proactive, I advised my mother that I would increase her monthly allotment from $20 to $25. As expected, she sent a letter back to me and asked for a larger monthly increase. I never did respond to her request. I know that pissed her off.

As an E-5, I was now being paid over $350 a month, and this money was tax-free. I went to the personnel office and increased my monthly deposit in the 10 percent soldiers saving plan to $300 each month. I was successful in living off minimal money each month after I paid my Vietnamese barrack's maid.

Grandfather Little and Grandfather Gould always advised me to save money for a rainy day. Thanks to their advice, my goal was to have a hefty bank account when I rotated back to the "world."

However, I used my first monthly pay increase to sign up for seven days of rest and recuperation (R&R) in Hong Kong.

REST AND RECUPERATION (R&R) IN HONG KONG

I spent seven fun-loving days on R&R in Hong Kong. During the late 1960s, Hong Kong was still under British rule. The British had signed a one-hundred-year lease agreement with the Chinese to rule Hong Kong. After the one-hundred-year lease expired, the British would relinquish control of Hong Kong and return it to the Chinese.

In addition to Chinese, people from various ethnic groups lived in Hong Kong. There was an extremely large population of East Indians.

In addition to having fun drinking and dancing, I purchased a stylish wardrobe of tailor-made clothes. When I returned to Vietnam, I showed my soldier buddies my new wardrobe. They gave me nods of approval and congratulated me.

EXTENDING MY TOUR OF DUTY IN VIETNAM FOR SIX MONTHS

Daily fear of death was at the front of the minds of every soldier who served in Vietnam. Being on high alert and fearing death each day, seeing death and destruction, and other atrocities were factors that caused post-traumatic stress disorder (PTSD) in soldiers.

Factors that convinced me to extend my tour of duty in Vietnam included having (1) my five soldier buddies as my trusting friends (as previously mentioned, we were close, like blood brothers);

(2) a tax-free monthly salary; (3) a 10 percent soldiers saving plan; (4) a maid service in the barracks; (5) seven additional days of R&R; and (6) a free thirty days of leave (vacation) back in the USA.

In May 1970 in Vietnam, I talked to Master Sergeant Gibbs (E-8) about extending my Vietnam tour for another six months. I also requested reassignment to the message center's classified materials mail room and courier service. Staff delivered classified materials to the US American Embassy in Saigon and to United States and South Vietnamese military bases outside Saigon. Two of my soldier buddies worked in the office and really enjoyed working for their E-7 supervisor. His name was Sergeant First Class Bowen from Alabama.

My requests for reassignment to the mail room and six-month extension of duty in Vietnam were quickly approved. In June 1970, after spending thirteen months in Vietnam, I received military orders and flew from South Vietnam to San Francisco, California. I also booked a second flight from San Francisco to Charlotte, North Carolina, to begin my thirty days' military leave. I was so over-whelmed with joy to be going home. The grueling twenty-one-hour flight back to the USA seemed insignificant.

On the flight home, flight attendants served homeward-bound soldiers delicious steak dinners, succulent side dishes, and mouthwatering desserts. Nonalcoholic beverages were free flowing. Soldiers celebrated their happiness by talking loudly, laughing, and playing loud music. Every soldier on the airplane had a big smile on his face.

LANDING AT THE SAN FRANCISCO, CALIFORNIA, AIRPORT IN JUNE 1970

After several refueling stops, the airplane finally landed in San Francisco, California. Soldiers cheered after flight attendants opened the airplane's doors. Some soldiers kissed the ground after they exited the airplane.

The soldiers' jubilant celebration for arriving safely back into the USA soon ended abruptly. As we entered the airport, we were met with a large group of protesters carrying signs that displayed end the war in Vietnam! They threw raw eggs, spat on us, cursed and called us baby killers. We ran fast to avoid the protesters. We secured our duffel bags and lined up to go through customs.

RACIST CUSTOMS OFFICER

In 1970, while I stood in the customs inspection line, a customs officer approached me and told me to grab my duffel bag and follow him. We walked into an empty room, and he told me to empty my clothes out of the duffel bag onto the floor. I complied with his request. He walked over and kicked my clothes around. I asked, "What are you looking for?" In a loud voice, he said, "You fit the profile of a drug dealer." I laughed, and it pissed him off. We had a brief staring contest, and because he did not find any illegal drugs, he shouted, "I hope you don't like it, because I brought you in here!" My military training taught me to keep my cool under trying situations. I packed my duffel bag and thought to myself, I have not been back into the USA but a few minutes, and a racist customs officer is trying to provoke me. I grabbed my duffel bag and walked out of the room.

Just as I got back in line, Major Bowles (the military officer in charge of soldiers returning from Vietnam) approached me, looked at my uniform name tag, and said, "Where have you been, Specialist Little?" I responded, "Sir, a customs officer pulled me out of line, searched my duffel bag, and accused me of being a drug dealer." The major said, "Point him out, Little!" I gladly pointed out the short man with a big ego. Major Bowles walked over to him and shouted, "Make this your last time you ever harass my soldiers returning home from Vietnam!" The customs officer's face turned red, and he sheepishly said, "Yes, sir." Soldiers gave Major Bowles a loud applause, and we continuously thanked him for defending us. Customs officers often racially profiled black soldiers.

Okay, let's fast-forward to summer 2015. As a mature civilian, I processed through the Thurgood Marshall Airport to catch a flight to Fort Lauderdale to board a cruise ship. After I successfully processed through the scanning machine, I encountered a short racist redneck Transportation Security Administration (TSA) officer. He called me to the side and said, "Let me check your pants legs. I just need to make sure you are not wearing a monitor." I was livid and went straight to his supervisor. His supervisor thought the incident was funny. I let the situation go as I was in a hurry to catch my flight. Plus, life has taught me, if this bold racist behavior is accepted at the TSA working level, it is promoted by upper managers who are also racist. Sometimes it is better to let God handle racists.

MY FLIGHT FROM SAN FRANCISCO, CALIFORNIA, TO CHARLOTTE, NORTH CAROLINA

After clearing customs, soldiers went their separate ways. Vietnam veterans did not receive welcome-home parades or celebrations. I threw my duffel bag across my shoulder and ran to catch my next flight from San Francisco, California, to Charlotte, North Carolina. I telephoned my father while in San Francisco and gave him the time my flight would arrive in Charlotte. When I arrived, he was standing in the airport, waiting with a big smile on his face. This was one of a few tender moments I experienced with my father.

It was a forty-five-minute drive home from Charlotte, North Carolina, to New London, North Carolina. During the drive, my father said it was hard being a soldier in a war zone. He said, "It forces you to grow up fast. You quickly become a man and learn how to protect yourself."

His comment brought a thought to the forefront of my mind. This thought resonated in my head from May 1969, when my father drove me to the bus station in Salisbury, North Carolina, until June 1970, when I arrived in Charlotte. I reminded my father of his comment to me at the bus station in May 1969. I quoted his words. "Boy, follow the sergeant's orders, and you will come back home safely."

I asked him, "How did you know I would make it back home safely?"

He responded, "I just knew you would come back home safely, as I raised you to be a responsible, thinking man."

I took that statement as a compliment and smiled.

THIRTY DAYS MILITARY LEAVE IN NEW LONDON, NORTH CAROLINA

When we arrived home, I went into my mother's bedroom to say hello. She pretended to be asleep. I said, "I have some money for you." She immediately sat up in the bed and wanted to talk. Shortly thereafter, I went into my old bedroom to unpack my duffel bag. I brought home all the tailor-made clothes I purchased in Hong Kong. I intended to make a fashion statement while at home.

The next day, I drove the family car to Mount Gilead, North Carolina, to visit Grandfather and Grandmother Little and Aunt Ellen. As always, I received a loving welcome and delicious, home-made food. They said, "We prayed for you while you were in Vietnam." I thanked them. I felt so overwhelmed with their love.

I sat down on the living room floor beside Grandmother Little as she sat in a straight-back straw chair. As I had done numerous times in past years, I laid my head on her lap without saying a word.

It was so soothing and comforting the way she lovingly rubbed my head. Her bottom lip was full of Old Navy snuff. Every now and then, she picked up an old tin can to spit liquid snuff out of her mouth.

After I finished eating the delicious food, Grandfather Little said, "Boy, meet me outside by the woodpile to cut some firewood. He then asserted, "You know, boy, I am still trying to make a man out of you." Starting as far back as to when I was eight, he continued to give me a lecture on being a responsible man. Grandfather Little was now around eighty and still had a sharp mind.

GRANDFATHER LITTLE WANTED TO BUY BEER FOR HIS ARTHRITIS

Just as I was about to leave, Grandfather Little asked, "Boy, do you mind driving me to the store?" Just as I was backing the car out of the sand-covered driveway, he gave me instruction on how to drive and directions to the country store. His directions were in the opposite direction of the country store. He really wanted me to drive to the beer store.

Finally, he said, "Boy, take me to the beer garden (store) to buy a six-pack of beer. My arthritis is flaring up. Do not mention this to your grandmother, because I don't want to hear her fussing about me drinking a beer. She won't believe I am using beer as medicine for my arthritis."

I bought a six-pack of beer for my grandfather. It was funny seeing him with a can opener in his pocket. He opened the first can of beer and drank it quickly. After releasing a loud burp, he asked, "Boy, would you like a cold beer?" I smiled and replied, "No, sir." He opened a second can of beer and drank it slowly. He started feeling the effects of the alcohol about halfway home.

When we arrived home, Grandfather Little said, "Do not drive up into the yard. Just let me out by the side of the road. Thank you, boy, for buying the beer. It will help my arthritis. Do not mention the beer to your grandmother. When I drink beer, it makes her mad, because I am the superintendent of the church." I smiled and said, "Okay." My grandfather got out of the car and walked at a steady pace toward the outdoor toilet. He had four beers tucked away under his arm. He probably fell asleep in the outdoor toilet after drinking the remaining four beers. I drove away quickly as I did not want to answer Grandmother Little's questions about the beer, I bought for Grandfather Little.

CHAPTER 39

MY TRAUMATIC HEAD INJURY FROM A HORRIBLE CAR ACCIDENT

It was in mid-June 1970, the first two weeks of my military leave. I decided to ride as a passenger to visit friends who lived in Durham, North Carolina. During a heavy rain on Interstate 85, a drunk driver crossed the median strip and caused a seven-car accident. I was riding in a car with bucket seats, and I was a passenger in the back seat. When I saw our car about to rear-end the car in front, I moved forward between the bucket seats and attempted to pull the car's steering wheel to the right to avoid hitting the car, but without success. At impact, my head went under the car's dashboard.

I was taken by ambulance to Duke University Hospital for a physical examination and x-rays. A doctor (neurologist) reviewed my head x-rays and concluded that I had sustained a serious skull fracture. The doctor was preparing to do surgery on me when hospital staff advised him that I was on active duty with the US Army. Since Duke was a private hospital, I was transferred to the closest federal medical center, Durham's Veterans Affairs Medical Center (VAMC).

SUCCESSFUL SKULL FRACTURE SURGERY

Since the Durham VAMC was a teaching medical center, I begged the Duke neurologist named Dr. Spencer to perform my head surgery. He consented to do my surgery since he had medical privileges at the VA Medical Center. We shook hands on our deal.

When I woke up from the anesthesia, Dr. Spencer told me the skull fracture surgery was successful. He said he removed roughly two inches of bone from the right side of my head along with a small portion of my brain. He further stated, "I want you to stay in the Durham VAMC for at least two more weeks for observation and follow-up examinations. Before I was discharged from the Durham VAMC, Dr. Spencer ordered me to stay home for two more weeks and to subsequently report to the Fayetteville Army Hospital for clearance to go back on active duty.

After my two-week stay in the Durham VAMC, my father drove two hours from New London to Durham to drive me home. When I arrived, my mother showed no emotion regarding my head injury. She commented, "You were a fool before your head injury, and I know you do not have any common sense now!" Since I was four, when I had rheumatic fever, she always harassed me about my poor health. I took her comment in stride and did not respond. She did; however, try to engage me in a conversation regarding collecting insurance money for the car accident. I told her I had to get ready to go back to Vietnam.

MY MEDICAL EXAMINATION AT FAYETTEVILLE, NORTH CAROLINA, ARMY HOSPITAL

Two weeks later, I drove two hours to report to the Fayetteville Army Hospital for a fit-for-military-duty medical evaluation. After the evaluation, the military doctor named Captain James told me to stay home for two more weeks, and after that time, I could return to active duty. He then asked, "Where would you like to be stationed?" Before I responded, the doctor said, "Specialist Little, based on the serious nature of your head injury, I can assign you to your next duty station." I said, "Sir, I would like to go back to my unit in Vietnam. Sir, my soldier buddies are there, waiting for me." Captain James raised his voice and said, "You want to do what?" I begged him, "Sir, please send me back to Vietnam!" Showing frustration, the doctor told me, "I can send you to Hawaii." I responded, "With all due respect, sir, please send me back to Vietnam." He asserted, "Specialist Little, for the last time, I have the authority to send you to any military base in the world." I repeated, "Sir, I just want to go back to Vietnam."

Captain James and I went back and forth regarding my request to go back to Vietnam. Finally, he said, "Okay, I will authorize you to go back to Vietnam. But you have to sign a statement indicating I gave you options for other military duty stations and you refused." He shook his head and said, "You sure are adamant about going back to Vietnam." After I signed the statement, the doctor shook my hand, smiled, and said, "You are one stubborn soldier!"

With a puzzled look on his face, Captain James remarked, "Most soldiers would jump at the opportunity to be stationed anywhere in the world. But okay, I cleared you for duty in Vietnam. Be safe, Little!" Captain James then said that he would notify my unit in Vietnam that I will report for duty in two weeks. He gave me a signed copy of my medical release form to give to my commanding officer in Vietnam. I happily responded, "Thank you, sir!"

Two major side effects I frequently encounter from my skull fracture are painful migraine headaches and neck pain. Regardless of my conditions, I was determined to keep pursuing my dreams and visions for a better life.

CHAPTER 40

REPORTING FOR DUTY IN VIETNAM

Two weeks later, I reported to my old unit in Vietnam. I let my hair grow out to hide my skull fracture scar. I had a teeny-weeny afro (TWA) hairstyle. Around this time, the commanding general for Vietnam tried to improve race relations in the army. Racial tensions were very high in Vietnam, and because of this, black and white soldiers were shooting one another at an alarming rate. Infantry soldiers discussed this situation openly in Saigon bars. In some bars downtown, the South Vietnamese catered only to white soldiers. This discrimination also increased racial tensions.

At one time, soldiers could walk around Downtown Saigon with loaded M16 rifles. Because of racial tension, the commanding officer restricted soldiers from carrying loaded rifles in Saigon.

The commanding general soon ordered that black soldiers could now wear afro hairstyles; however, a soldier's hair could not exceed three inches in length. He also ordered commissaries (military stores) to stock afro hair-care and shaving products for black soldiers with ingrown facial hair. Lastly, he ordered the enlisted club to hire bands to play soul or funky music. Prior to the general's order, enlisted clubs' bands played mostly country music for white soldiers.

When I reported to my barracks, my Vietnamese maid, named Huang, ran and jumped into my arms. She said, "You are my number one GI (soldier), and I missed you!" She then asked, "Are you okay?" I responded, "Yes, and thank you for asking." Although I was away in the USA for almost two months, I gave her two months' back pay. My good will gesture really made her happy.

MY NEW DUTY STATION

After I changed from my military dress uniform into my jungle fatigues and boots, I walked over to my new duty station in the mail room. The soldiers in the mail room froze in place and stared at me. Captain Jones, who oversaw the mail room, ran out of his office and walked close to me to read the name tag on my fatigue shirt. His behavior made me nervous.

He then said, "Specialist Little, we received a report from the Fayetteville, North Carolina, army hospital that you were killed in a car accident."

I said, "Sir, I was involved in a car accident, but as you can see, I am still alive." Captain Jones asserted, "It's a good thing you reported for duty today, as I was directed to cut locks off your wall and footlockers in the barracks and to mail your personal belongings to your home address." He shook my hand and welcomed me back.

News traveled fast, and eventually, I was surrounded by my old and new coworkers and my soldier buddies. They, too, welcomed me back to Vietnam. Captain Jones gave me the rest of the day off and to get settled in the barracks. I thanked him for the time off. I was scheduled to report for duty at seven the next morning.

REUNION WITH MY SOLDIER BUDDIES

After eating lunch at the military mess hall (cafeteria), I returned to the barracks to finish unpacking my duffel bag (military suitcase). Feeling tired, I pulled off my boots and took a nap on my bunk bed.

Later that evening, my soldier buddies stood near my bunk and poured beer on my face to wake me up. They insisted that I come down the hall as they had several cases of beer to celebrate my safe return. They had fun laughing at me that night. One soldier asked, "Little, how can you spend thirteen months in Vietnam and not get injured? But while you are safe in the USA, you almost got killed!" Go figure! My soldier buddies laughed out of control at me. I laughed, shrugged my shoulders, and opened another can of beer.

MY NEW JOB ASSIGNMENT IN THE MAIL ROOM

When I reported for work at seven the next morning, I met my new supervisor, a white sergeant first class (E-7) from Alabama. Sergeant Bowen and I immediately established an excellent relationship. He was a no-nonsense supervisor but was extremely fair to soldiers who worked for him. He required us to report to work on time and to go beyond the call of duty in performing job assignments.

MAIL COURIER TEAM LEADER

On my first day on the job with the mail room, Sergeant Bowen told me that we were responsible for delivering highly classified mail to the American Embassy in Saigon and to United

States and South Vietnamese military bases outside Saigon. He also told me to ride along with the courier team to observe the operation. He especially wanted me to pay close attention to the caution the team took to safeguard highly classified mail. He then explained that I would make two courier deliveries each day, one in the morning and another in the afternoon. He underscored that I should always be mindful of my surroundings while driving on courier routes as danger was always lurking.

Sergeant Bowen then directed me to join the courier team at the mailboxes to learn how to sort mail by mail delivery stops and help load crates of classified mail into a large gray suburban truck parked outside the building. He asked me to come back to see him after the team finished loading the truck.

He was adamant an armed soldier must always remain in the truck when delivering classified mail. He then told me to sign a military form to check out an M16 rifle, two belts of extra M16 bullets to drape around my neck and shoulders, and a .45-caliber pistol with a holster with extra bullets to wear around my waist. Sergeant Bowen said, "This is your daily uniform."

After one week of my riding along and delivering mail, Sergeant Bowen appointed me as the new E-5 or team leader for the mail courier team. He said I would have three soldiers on my team with the rank of private first class (E-3). Their names were James, Roger, and Arthur. I had already met the three soldiers during the one-week ride along. He said I would also have a truck driver from Laos named Tick reporting to me and he has a security clearance.

In a stern voice, Sergeant Bowen said, "You are responsible for your team's safety and well-being and, more importantly, the security of classified mail. Lastly, if you lose any classified mail, you will go to a military jail, or better yet, do not come back. I am serious, Little!" These last two statements from Sergeant Bowen left a huge lump in my throat.

MY FIRST MAIL COURIER TRIP

On my first trip, I tried to act like a brave soldier leading his men. On the inside, my heart was pounding. I took the safety off my M16 rifle and had it pointing toward the truck's window and ready to fire at the enemy. I also laid my .45-caliber pistol on the seat beside me just in case.

The streets were crowded with numerous Vietnamese, who were either walking, riding motorbikes, or driving taxicabs. Since there were only a few sidewalks, everyone crowded into the streets. My Laotian truck driver, named Tick, had to be very careful in maneuvering the truck through people and traffic. The weather was hot, and the air was full of smog.

As I observed the Vietnamese, I pondered on who looked friendly and who did not. Some Vietnamese wore civilian clothes and openly carried firearms. Trying to survey this new environment tied my brain into a knot. My stress level in the truck went through the ceiling. I thought, Welcome to guerrilla warfare, Ken!

During the first mail stop, I got out of the truck and scanned the environment to ensure safety of my three-man team—James, Arthur, and Roger—and the classified mail. I went into the building with James to observe the process for delivering mail. As I exited the building, I was on high alert again, checking the environment. I walked slowly to get back into the truck.

The E-5 or former team leader, named Chuck, whom I replaced, was also riding in the truck. After my first stop in delivering mail, Chuck gave me advice on my new team leader role. He said, "Little, please stop being on such high alert—your fatigues are soaking wet with sweat! You need to relax but continue to be mindful of your environment. Please put the safety back on your M16 rifle and keep the .45-caliber pistol in your holster. Next, please roll down your window so air can circulate through the truck."

One of the rules of engagement while delivering mail was, you must be faced with "clear and present danger" before using your firearms. The army trained us to detect clear and present danger. We did not want to shoot innocent people just because they looked suspicious. Most of the people we encountered were friendly, hardworking people. Sometimes they approached the truck just to say hello or try to sell handmade products.

As we learned in the army's orientation program for new soldiers entering Vietnam, we were guests in Vietnam and we must govern ourselves accordingly.

Based on Chuck's advice from that day forward, I toned down my alertness just a little. I was always mindful of Sergeant Bowen's warning on my first day on the job. "If you lose any classified mail, you will go to military jail, or better yet, do not come back!" His warning kept me motivated to protect my team and the classified mail. I just wanted to do a good job.

CHAPTER 41

CARE PACKAGE IN THE MAIL FROM MY MOTHER

To my surprise, one day I received a care package from my mother. It was a cardboard box full of cookies, doughnuts, honey buns, and candy. I shared the goodies with my soldier buddies that night. That night, while lying in my bunk bed, I asked myself, "Why is my mother being nice to me?"

Well, the answer to that question showed up in a letter from my mother several days later. It was another one of her games to demand money from me. Looking back, right after I arrived in Germany, she wrote me a letter demanding $250 to buy new car tires since I drove the car while on military leave in New London, North Carolina.

It was like history repeated itself with my mother. She once again demanded $250 from me to buy new car tires since I drove the car while on military leave before returning to Vietnam. As I did in Germany, I did not respond to her demand for $250. Her greed for money continued to annoy me.

AN "OH MY GOD" (OMG) LETTER FROM MY MOTHER

A month later, I received another letter from my mother. She wrote, "I hope you get killed in Vietnam so I can collect the $10,000 from your military insurance policy." My first reaction to her letter was "Oh my God!" I was traumatized after reading her letter. I read the letter again to make sure she wanted me to get killed in Vietnam just to collect insurance money. Her letter caused pain to deeply penetrate my heart and soul. A steady stream of tears rolled from my eyes and saturated my face and my military fatigues (clothes).

My immediate thought was, *I hate my mother for writing this letter!* As the old saying goes, "this was the straw that broke the camel's back!" My memory started playing back my mother's numerous mean deeds toward me dating back to when I was aged three.

Driven by my emotions, I sat down and wrote my mother a five-page letter detailing a lot of her mean deeds toward me. I specifically stated that I hate Mr. Pimp with a passion and the numerous other men with whom she had extramarital affairs. I strongly emphasized that I hoped I'd never marry a woman like her.

How odd. Just as I was about to mail the letter to my mother, the words to Grandmother Little's life lesson echoed in my mind. When I was eight, as we were walking on the road going fishing in Mount Gilead, she said, "Baby, always respect your parents regardless of the situation." I guess Grandmother Little knew it was inevitable this day would come during my lifetime. I later burned the horrible letter I had written my mother. Writing that horrible letter to my mother ended up being a form of therapy for me. Temporarily, the letter helped me flush out bad memories I retained in my head and heart regarding my mother.

Is it possible to love your mother and strongly dislike her character? Strangely enough, my mother never allowed anyone other than herself to abuse me. This was due to my mother's untreated mental health issue.

Later that night, I joined my soldier buddies to drink beer and listened to loud music.

REST AND RECUPERATION (R&R)

After being back in Vietnam for several months, I went to Sydney, Australia, on R&R. This was a never-ending, week long party. Live bands played the latest soul and funky music in clubs. The dance floor was always filled with Australians and American soldiers dancing, singing, and having fun. I dressed up in the stylish, tailor-made clothes I purchased in Hong Kong on R&R.

There were beautiful aboriginal women in the club. They could really dance. Aborigines are brown-skinned people who were the early inhabitants of Australia until they were invaded and colonized by the British.

The Australians were gracious and treated American soldiers with respect. During the day, I went sightseeing in Sydney. I ate great-tasting food in restaurants, visited museums, walked through beautiful parks, and explored along the beautiful waterfront. Overall, I had a beautiful time in Sydney, Australia.

GOOD NEWS

When I returned to Vietnam from Australia, I received good news from my supervisor. He announced that the army issued orders granting early separations from the military for soldiers who were within six months of separating from active duty. My supervisor made that announcement in early November 1970.

I quickly calculated the number of months I had left on active duty with the army. Since I was scheduled to be separated from the army in April 1971, my separation date fell within that six-month window. I immediately broke out into a happy dance in the mail room. My team members laughed at me acting silly. I asked my supervisor, "What is the procedure for getting the early separation?" He directed me to do my morning mail courier run, take the afternoon off, and go to the military personnel office to complete paperwork requesting early separation. I was happy to comply with my supervisor's instructions.

Within a week, I received military orders granting me early separation from the army in mid-December 1970. That night, I bought two cases of beer to celebrate my early separation from the army with my soldier buddies. We also went to Downtown Saigon to celebrate with the ladies. I looked forward to celebrating Christmas at home in North Carolina.

One night in the barracks, while I was alone with my thoughts, I thought about leaving my soldier buddies in December. It made me sad knowing I would leave them behind. Through adversity and good times, we were always there for one another. I would miss their friendship and brotherhood.

DECENT PROPOSAL

As I was preparing to go out on my afternoon courier mail run, the master sergeant (E-8) called me into his office. Immediately, I started praying that my early separation orders had not been rescinded. It was quite the contrary; the master sergeant made me a decent proposal. He said, "Little, I would like you to stay in Vietnam and work for me until your original enlistment date expires in April 1971. I will send you home for thirty days military leave for

Christmas and recommend you for promotion from specialist fifth class [E-5] to staff sergeant [E-6]." This was a generous offer from the E-8. I politely asked the E-8 if I could think about his proposal and give him an answer the next morning. He agreed.

That night, I shared the E-8's proposal with my soldier buddies. They reminded me that since we connected in Vietnam, I had always talked about my dream of enrolling in a four-year college and earning a degree. They recommended that I take the early separation from the army for Christmas. They also encouraged me to use the GI Bill to fulfill my dream of going to college and earning a college degree.

They also suggested that after I earned a college degree, I should re-enlist in the military and come back as a commissioned officer (second lieutenant). The E-8 would then have to salute and address me as sir. It was group consensus that I should go home, pursue my dream of enrolling in a four-year college or university, and earn a college degree.

The next day, I thanked the E-8 for his offer for me to stay in Vietnam and get promoted to E-6. I told him; however, I had always dreamed of going to a four-year college or university to earn a degree. I would like to pursue my dream.

LEAVING VIETNAM AND SEPARATING FROM THE ARMY

On my last day in Vietnam, my soldier buddies rode the bus with me to the military airport to say goodbye. It was an emotional moment saying goodbye to my soldier buddies. It is still interesting to me how adverse conditions can create a bond among soldiers. To date, I have not bonded with a group of people in civilian life like I did with my soldier buddies in Vietnam. That bond was built on trust.

On December 18, 1970, I separated from the army in San Francisco, California. Again, soldiers were greeted by many people protesting the Vietnam conflict. The protesters did not bother me too much this time as I was focused on separating from the army, getting paid, and flying home to celebrate Christmas.

Military staff offered us a free ride to the airport on a military bus. However, they said, "You guys must wait for at least an hour." Someone in my group yelled out, "An empty taxicab is outside!" Eight of us former soldiers jammed our duffel bags into the taxicab's trunk and crowded inside. We split the taxicab fare to the airport eight ways, shook hands, and went our separate ways in the airport.

FLYING FROM SAN FRANCISCO, CALIFORNIA, TO CHARLOTTE, NORTH CAROLINA

I found a pay telephone in the airport, called my father, and asked him to pick me up in Charlotte, North Carolina, later that afternoon. When I walked through the gate, again, he stood there with a big wide smile on his face. His smile appeared to be of happiness and relief of seeing me arrive home safely from Vietnam for a second time. This was a tender moment.

I was happy to be separated from the army and safely back in New London, North Carolina. In fact, I felt like a kid in a candy store. During the forty-five-minute drive from Charlotte, I told my father I saved a large sum of money in Vietnam and I wanted to buy a new car. He agreed to support me in searching for a new car.

When we arrived home, I received a chilly reception from my mother. I guess she was unhappy that I did not get killed in Vietnam so she could collect the $10,000 military insurance. Mentally, I dismissed her mean behavior.

MY FIRST NEW CAR

Since Christmas was seven days away, I focused on buying a new car and having fun. The next day, my father drove me to different car dealerships. Finally, I found a brand-new 1971 Plymouth GTX. It was a super fast car. It was beautiful as it had a white body, a black vinyl top, black leather bucket seats, and manual four-speed gearshift in the floor.

Initially, I intended to pay cash for my new car with money I saved in Vietnam, but my father asked me to loan him some money and, in turn, he would make my monthly car payments to repay the loan. I complied with his request. My father made monthly car payments as promised.

It was a great feeling to purchase my first new car. Since I was twenty-two years old, I did not need a parent's signature authorizing me to buy my car. I did have a flashback to 1967, when I called from Newport News, Virginia, and asked my mother to sign for me to get a new car. I had saved $500 to purchase a new car. My mother blackmailed me and threatened to persuade Grandfather Gould to put me out of his house if I did not send her my $500. In hindsight, although I was angry with my money-grubbing mother, I realized her blackmailing me became a blessing in disguise. After I joined the army, I did not have enough money to make car payments anyway from my private E-1 monthly military salary of $97.50.

A BONEHEAD MOVE

I made another bonehead move of involving my mother with my money. The excitement of being home from Vietnam caused me to have a lapse in judgment. One night, before going out to party, I realized I had $1,500 cash in my pockets. In a hurry to go out to party, I asked my mother to hold my $1,500 for a few days until I could open a savings account. This was the biggest and most expensive bonehead move I ever made with my mother.

A few days later, I asked my mother for my money. She gave me $500. I asked, "Where is the rest of my money?" I told her $1,000 was missing. She raised her voice and yelled, "Fool, I gave you that money! Are you on drugs?"

I just stood there and gave her a deep, dark stare. My stare made her very nervous. Finally, I went into the bedroom, packed my clothes, and left the house. I was angry with myself for making the bonehead move of trusting my mother with my money.

After I calmed down from my anger, I decided to drive back to Newport News, Virginia, that night and check in with my old job at the Newport News Shipyard. On the way, I decided to take a detour and pay Mandy a surprise visit at college.

CHAPTER 42

VISITING MANDY AT COLLEGE

The purpose of my visit was to sincerely apologize to Mandy for the way I treated her while in Newport News regarding Terri and other women. When I arrived at the college, it was perfect timing that night—Mandy marched by me in a line with other young ladies. She was pledging a sorority.

When our eyes met, she gave me a big smile. She asked her big sister in charge of the line pledgees if she could say hello to her boyfriend who just returned home from Vietnam. The big sister dismissed all pledgees and told them to have a merry Christmas and happy New Year. Mandy ran over, jumped into my arms, and kissed me. She smiled and introduced me to her pledgee sisters as her boyfriend.

After her pledgee sisters walked away, Mandy asked me to take her out to eat as she was starving. We drove to a run-down club, and I bought some delicious fried chicken sandwiches. We drenched the fried chicken in hot sauce.

I later told Mandy I was driving to Newport News that night to report to work at the shipyard after New Year's Day (1971). She asked, "Do you mind if I ride home with you? My clothes are already packed, as I planned to catch the bus to go home early tomorrow morning."

We went back to campus, secured her luggage, and drove for six hours to Newport News. Along the way, we laughed and talked the whole time. She even joked with me about Terri getting married and having a baby while I was away in the military. I laughed on the outside, but inside, my heart yearned for Terri.

We arrived in Newport News around four the next morning. Mandy said she did not want to disturb my family this early in the morning and suggested we drive to Bay Shore Beach in Hampton, Virginia, park, and watch the sun rise. As we drove toward the beach, I felt sleepy. I told Mandy I needed to check into a hotel to get some sleep. She said, "Okay!" We drove to a hotel on the waterfront in Norfolk, Virginia.

After we checked into a hotel, we took turns taking a shower. I dozed off to sleep while Mandy was in the shower. She woke me up after she came out of the shower. I went in and took a quick hot shower. When I came out, she was lying on the bed, completely nude. Suddenly, after looking at her beautiful body, I was rejuvenated and ready to make love. We made passionate love for a long time. In fact, we were making love as the sun rose over the waterfront.

Around 11:00 a.m., we checked out of the hotel and went to a restaurant to eat breakfast. Around 1:00 p.m., we arrived at our homes on Hampton Avenue in Newport News. Several hours later, Mandy came over to talk to Grandfather and Grandmother Gould.

Later, Mandy and I went into the living room to talk. She moved close to me and whispered, "My parents heard the loud sound of your car's mufflers when we arrived at four this morning. They wanted to know where we were since that time. I told them that I did not want to disturb them that early in the morning so we drove to Bay Shore Beach in Hampton, Virginia, to watch the sunrise. The next lie I told them was we fell asleep in the car waiting for the sun to rise. When we woke up, we went to breakfast and sat and talked for a long time. Make sure you repeat these same lies if they ask you."

REPORTING TO WORK AT THE SHIPYARD IN NEWPORT NEWS, VIRGINIA

I did not want to make the same mistake my father made when he came home from Germany after World War II. He did not immediately report back to Alcoa after separating from the army. This caused him to lose seniority with the company.

I reported to work a few days after New Year's Day in 1971. After spending several hours in personnel filling out paperwork, I was sent to an aircraft carrier to support a sheet metal mechanic installing air ventilation. This was the same job assignment I had before I enlisted in the army in 1968. It was dark, damp, and cold on the aircraft carrier. I shivered as I wore dressy clothes and shoes instead of heavy-duty, steel-toed shoes and warm work clothes.

After several hours, I did a self-examination and asked myself if I wanted a job to perform hard, manual labor. Did I want a job using my brains and not my muscle? I asked myself, "What happened to your dreams and visions of going to a four-year college or university to earn a bachelor's degree?"

I immediately walked over to the mechanic and told him this was no reflection on him but I was resigning from the shipyard and enrolling in college. I shook his hand and walked up to personnel to resign. It took two hours for staff to process me out. They had to pay me for the few hours I worked that morning and vacation time I accrued while in the army. I also closed my credit union account.

I went back home and packed my clothes. I told my grandparents I resigned from the shipyard and was driving back to North Carolina to enroll in college. Before departing, I shook

Grandfather Gould's hand and thanked him for getting me a job in the shipyard. He said, "Grandboy, you are making the right decisions. Get your college education and find a high-paying job." Grandmother Gould gave me a smile and a big hug and wished me well. Lastly, I thanked both for sharing their home with me.

MY SEARCH FOR A FOUR-YEAR COLLEGE OR UNIVERSITY

During my drive from Newport News, I made several stops at four-year colleges and universities in North Carolina. I was looking for in-state tuition since my home address was in North Carolina. In-state tuition would be less expensive and would allow me to retain extra money from my monthly GI Bill education check.

Since I never attended a four-year college or university, I was not familiar with their acceptance and enrollment processes. My only experience with college was enrolling in Peninsula Business College (PBC) in Newport News, Virginia. When I enrolled in PBC, I walked into the school, paid my money, and immediately became a PBC student.

I used this same approach to enroll in several four-year colleges and universities in North Carolina and got rejected. University staff told me to apply and they would notify me later regarding acceptance. Plus, they said it was too late to enroll in the spring 1971 semester. I was deeply disappointed. My next stop was to find a job, stay at home in New London, North Carolina, and start school during the 1971 fall semester.

MY VISIT TO
THE EMPLOYMENT OFFICE
IN ALBEMARLE, NORTH CAROLINA

My first encounter was with a white staff member who was adamant about sending me on interviews for jobs such as a dishwasher, janitor, and other low-paying jobs. During that time, these were stereotype jobs for "colored only." I gave him a lot of pushback as I was adamant about not interviewing for low-paying jobs. Since we were at a stalemate, I ventured out and started looking for employment at major manufacturing companies.

Eventually, I interviewed and got an administrative job working for a local major manufacturing company in Albemarle, North Carolina. The job entailed working in an office computing mathematical formula to dye industrial carpet. I worked five nights per week from 11:00 p.m. to 7:00 a.m. I wore business attire to work and did not get my clothes or hands dirty.

When I reported to work on my first day, a white supervisor told me he didn't want to be my friend as he had problems with my kind (black people). He told me to just do my work and stay out of his way. I reached out and shook his hand and said, "You have a deal." He was really trying to provoke me to say something negative. I thought to myself, this job is just a stepping stone to higher dreams and visions for my future. I worked for this company from February to August 1971.

APPLYING TOO LATE FOR ACCEPTANCE
AT COLLEGES AND UNIVERSITIES

Along with working, I spent a lot of time having fun from February to August 1971. I allowed time to apply for school to expire. Feeling disappointed with myself, I packed my suitcases and drove back to Newport News, Virginia, and moved in with Grandfather and Grandmother Gould. A few days later, I asked my uncle Jason if I could leave my new car at his house as I was moving to New York with his daughter (my first cousin).

CHAPTER 43

MOVING AND LIVING IN NEW YORK

In August 1971, I moved in with my cousin who lived in Bronx, New York. She allowed me to sleep on her living room couch as a temporary layover. Several weeks had passed, and I was running short on money. I remembered my job at the manufacturing company owed me two weeks' back pay. Before I resigned, the personnel staff said I would receive my last paycheck in the mail in two weeks. I verified my home address in New London, North Carolina, for them.

MY LAST PAYCHECK VANISHED

Two weeks later, I called and asked my mother, "Did the manufacturing company mail my paychecks to the house?" She answered no. I called personnel staff and asked, "Did you send my paychecks to my home address in New London?" The staff informed me, "Ken, we mailed your paycheck to your home address last week."

Feeling frustrated, I called my mother again and told her personnel staff told me they mailed my paycheck to the house last week. When my mother started cursing at me about the paycheck, that confirmed my suspicion—she had received and cashed my paycheck.

That was another mistake I made in dealing with my mother. I should have called personnel staff and gave them my new address in New York. My mother stole money I saved in Vietnam and now my paycheck. I briefly considered calling the Albemarle, North Carolina, police to report my paycheck as stolen. Again, Grandmother Little's words to me at the age of eight resonated in my head. "Baby, honor your mother and father regardless of the situation."

I decided not to call the police, because my mother would have ended up in jail. Going to jail would not have cured my mother's untreated mental health condition nor her greed for money. I am sure my mother had no regard for me being twenty-one years old, and my time as her indentured servant was over. From that time forward, I developed a strong dislike for lying, lazy, deadbeat thieves.

MY NEW JOB AND MY SHABBY ROOM IN AN APARTMENT

I later secured a job as a respiratory therapist trainee through a friend at a local hospital. I worked the evening shift, from 4:00 p.m. until 12:00 a.m. My cousin soon found me a room in a three-bed-room apartment in the Bronx. Two other tenants shared the kitchen, refrigerator, and bathroom with me. Sometimes my food disappeared from the kitchen cabinet and refrigerator. It was a shabby room in the apartment, but I viewed this room as a temporary layover.

NEW YORK'S FAST-PACED LIFE

I enjoyed the nightlife and entertainment in New York. I went to the world-famous Apollo Theater every week and enjoyed beautiful, soulful singing and dancing. The music and performances were captivating. My heart and soul embraced the beautiful, soul-stirring music.

I also enjoyed eating a variety of ethnic foods and wearing high-end contemporary clothes. I really enjoyed New York ladies, as they were bold and beautiful. I had fun dating and partying with New York ladies. I had matured and did not need to drink alcohol to communicate with these ladies.

DEFINING NIGHT IN MY LIFE

One night, I was out on a date with a beautiful, college-educated registered nurse. We worked at the same local hospital. She was of East Indian descent; however, she grew up in the West Indies island of Tobago. She was extremely intelligent and had an extensive vocabulary.

While we were out on a date, she used the word meticulous to describe one of my traits. I didn't know if the meaning of meticulous was good or bad. Feeling embarrassed, I asked her to define meticulous. That night was a defining moment in my life. The next day at work, I found a Webster's Dictionary and looked up the definition of meticulous. As noted in the dictionary, it means "extreme or excessive care in considering or treating details." Not knowing the definition of meticulous reminded me it was time to use my GI Bill education benefits. I had to commit myself to enrolling in a four-year college or university to pursue a bachelor's degree.

The fast-paced living in New York was also a challenge for me. I wondered if the fast-paced lifestyle, coupled with stress of attending a four-year college or university in New York, would overwhelm me. I concluded that a slower lifestyle in North Carolina would be a better environment to pursue an education. I embarked on the journey of applying to schools in North Carolina.

MY MENTAL FLASHBACKS IN NEW YORK OF BEING IN SAIGON, VIETNAM

I need to give a balanced evaluation of the time I lived in New York. While living there, I developed a sincere appreciation of the New York lifestyle. However, the downside of living in New York was the psychological strain it had on me. Oftentimes, I was on high mental alert traveling throughout the city. Day and night, New Yorkers were always moving fast. This city was not for people who were faint at heart, as a lot of New Yorkers were extremely rude. Sometimes I walked New York's noisy, people-crowded sidewalks; rode taxicabs on traffic-jammed streets, and stood up on people-packed commuter trains. These situations raised my anxiety level.

For example, one night, after I got off work, I was walking home in the Bronx. This was the night we received our paychecks at the local hospital. I rushed to leave work, go home to take a shower, change clothes, and go out on a date. I failed to change from the hospital uniform into my regular street clothes. This was a big mistake.

As I walked along the street, I noticed a car with two guys driving very slowly behind me. After I made eye contact with the guy on the passenger side, he jumped out and started running toward me. Still being physically army fit, I knew the fat slob would not catch me. The driver noticed his partner in crime was losing ground on me. He stopped and told him to get back into the car. They were burning rubber trying to catch me. As they were about to drive close to me in the car, I ran across the street. This was a one-way street with oncoming traffic. This one-way street with oncoming traffic allowed me to escape a mugging. Lesson learned: I never wore the hospital uniform in public again.

In Saigon, Vietnam, there was always an imminent threat of danger. In New York, the imminent threat of danger was low compared to Saigon. However, the fast-paced lifestyle in New York triggered flashbacks of me being back in Saigon, Vietnam. The garbage on New York streets stirred flashbacks. This pungent garbage odor reminded me of the rainy, smelly environment in Saigon.

In Saigon, my eyes constantly scanned extremely large crowds of people. I used this same behavior in large crowds in New York. Sometimes, my anticipation of violence in New York made me feel naked and insecure, especially amid large crowds of people. This was because I was not armed with my M16 rifle and .45-caliber pistol. These weapons served as my security blanket in Saigon.

CHAPTER 44

ACCEPTANCE AT A FOUR-YEAR UNIVERSITY

In January 1972, I applied for acceptance at several colleges and universities. In early spring 1972, I received my acceptance letter from North Carolina Central University (NCCU), a four-year, historically black university in Durham, North Carolina. In May 1972, I resigned from my job at the local hospital, packed my clothes, and caught the bus to Hampton, Virginia, to pick up my car at Uncle Jacob's house. After spending time with Uncle Jacob and Aunt Laney, I drove to Newport News to visit Grandfather and Grandmother Gould. I spent the evening talking to them about my plans of attending NCCU. They were so excited for me. The next morning, I drove to Durham, North Carolina.

MY UNIVERSITY LIFE EXPERIENCE

In late May 1972, I moved into an apartment in Durham. I secured a bellman's job at a local hotel. I made excellent tips handling hotel guests' luggage. I also drove the hotel's limousine to pick up or drop off hotel guests at the local airport.

I was required to work while I waited for my education checks to come in the mail from then Veterans Administration (VA), now Department of Veterans Affairs. The VA education checks often arrived on a sporadic schedule. Sometimes, VA education checks showed up in the middle or later in the month.

In June 1972, I started summer school classes as a freshman at North Carolina Central University (NCCU). My twenty-fourth birthday was in July. Initially, I felt like an old man surrounded by mostly eighteen-year-old students. That feeling soon passed after I met other Vietnam veterans in classes. I later joined the Veterans Club on campus.

It was a lengthy adjustment for me to develop solid study habits and attend classes regularly. These were my two biggest challenges at NCCU. In addition to working several odd jobs, my major distraction was being surrounded by numerous friendly, beautiful ladies.

After the first semester of my sophomore year, I finally made an adjustment to school. I learned to devote equal time to studying, attending classes, working odd jobs, and partying with the ladies.

One night, I was alone in my apartment when an old friend knocked on my door. She was attending another college in Durham. I knew her from our high school days. My West Badin High School classmates and I drove to Albemarle, North Carolina, to visit young ladies at their homes.

That night, alone in my apartment, I asked her for some romance. She suddenly broke out in tears and yelled, "I am afraid of you!" I backed away from her and asked why. She said, "Do you remember when you and your buddies used to come to my home in Albemarle to visit?" I answered yes. She said, "I never said anything to you, but my mother did not want you to come to my house." I responded, "What did I do to your mother?"

"It really wasn't about you; it was about your mother." She then told me a heartbreaking story about my mother. "Did you know my mother used to date Mr. Pimp?" I answered no. "My mother told me that your mother worked some witchcraft on her because she was involved with Mr. Pimp. My mother hated your mother so much that she did not want you coming to our house. Did you know your mother used witchcraft to chase other women away from Mr. Pimp?"

I told her my mother would never share any of her evil deeds with me. I vehemently told her, "I do not participate in evil, and I stay away from people who have a reputation for dabbling in it." I sincerely apologized to her for whatever my mother did to her mother.

We continued to be friends, and sometimes I gave her rides from school in Durham to her home in Albemarle. I never went inside her mother's house again. This was another embarrassing situation for me regarding my mother. Please help me, Jesus!

MARITAL BLISS

At the age of twenty-seven, I decided it was time to settle down. I married a beautiful young lady in December 1975. History repeated itself, and my mother strongly disapproved of the marriage. I ceased communicating with my mother for months as I was tired of her trying to ruin my relationship. I had had enough.

I established strong rapport with my wife's family. Her mother, a heavenly angel, will always have a place in my heart.

EARNING MY BACHELOR'S DEGREE

I completed class requirements for my bachelor's degree in December 1975 and graduated in May 1976. Overflowing with happiness, I called my mother to share the good news. Her response was "You will never be as smart as I am. I got my education living in New York City. Besides, your ass is too old to be in school. You need to get a blue-collar job to make money." Her responses were predictable; she was still of the illusion that she could take my hard-earned money as in the past. She could no longer say, "I can take every dollar you earn until you are twenty-one years old." My days as an indentured servant were over. I was over twenty-one years old. At the age of twenty-seven, I refused to continue to support her greed with my hard-earned money. I was emancipated. Free at last!

APPLYING FOR GRADUATE SCHOOL

I applied to two universities to pursue a master's degree. I got accepted at both schools: Clark University in Atlanta, Georgia, and the American University in Washington, DC. I decided to enroll in American University in Washington, DC. I had naive expectations of getting involved in politics. My wife was accepted in an undergraduate accounting program at Howard University in Washington, DC.

In July 1976, we moved from North Carolina to Arlington, Virginia. Even though our new apartment was roach infested, the rental cost in Arlington was almost double the rent we paid in North Carolina. The apartment complex did not have washing machines and dryers on-site. We packed our dirty laundry in bags and took it to the local Laundromats.

My wife and I commuted daily to the two different schools in Washington, DC. I pursued a master's degree, and she pursued a bachelor's degree.

To supplement my VA monthly education check, I worked part-time in American University's Veterans Affairs Office and received a small stipend. My wife secured a work-study job at

Howard University.

At times, we hardly had enough food to eat. To fight off hunger, we purchased commercial-size cans of mixed vegetables, and for months, we ate these vegetables three times a day. One day, we got a real treat. Two of my wife's brothers rode the bus from North Carolina to visit us in Arlington, Virginia. My mother-in-law had prepared fried chicken sandwiches for them to take on the trip. When they arrived at the bus station, they had leftover fried chicken sandwiches in a brown paper bag. We tore the bag open and ate the sandwiches within seconds. What a treat!

On a rare occasion, we went to our favorite Chinese restaurant in Arlington, Virginia. We bought one plate of food and shared it. This was another treat. Although we were poor, we mutually agreed to successfully complete our degree programs.

NEW FULL-TIME JOB

In late December 1977, I secured a blue-collar job with the US Postal Service as a mail carrier. It was challenging for me to attend graduate school and perform manual labor (heavy lifting and extensive walking) with the post office. I had to carry mail in different types of weather, such as cold, hot, rainy, snowy, and icy conditions.

After ninety days, I received a glowing performance review from my supervisor. I passed the probationary period and secured my job with the post office. I was now entitled to full-coverage health insurance. This was perfect timing, as my wife was pregnant and needed prenatal care.

We now searched for an affordable, clean, roach free two bedroom apartment located in a safe neighborhood. We found a con-temporary apartment in Alexandria, Virginia. One important luxury, the laundry room, was in the basement. We felt comfortable knowing our firstborn child would come home to a clean, modern apartment.

Very soon, we could buy new living room and bedroom furniture. We also bought our first new color television set. More importantly, we bought new baby furniture and decorated the second bedroom for our forthcoming new baby.

GREAT NEWS

I was thirty years old when I graduated from American University with a master's degree in August 1978. During my tenure at the school, I learned that my personal values did not fit into the cutthroat world of politics. However, this achievement moved me closer to realizing my dreams and visions for a better life.

I did not make it this far on my own. Thanks goes out to life lessons shared with me by green tree leaves on the tall tree in the backyard in New London, North Carolina; Mrs. Battle, my influential fourth-grade teacher; my father; Grandfather and Grandmother Little; Grandfather and Grandmother Gould; and the spirit of my dog, Skip. I would be remiss if I failed to mention my mother, as her mean spirit gave me strength and determination. These experiences prepared me to meet challenges head-on.

NEW BABY

In early 1979, it was a blessing to welcome our new baby girl. On doctor's orders, two nurses escorted me out of the delivery room as I tried to advise the doctor on how to deliver my daughter. In short, I was banned from the delivery room.

When the nurse brought my daughter out of the delivery room, she placed her in a room surrounded by glass with other newborn infants. Infants were isolated and secured within this glass-plated room. The nurse rolled her up front so I could see her through the glass. My new daughter was on her knees, with her eyes wide open. We stared at each other through the glass. I knew my precious, beautiful daughter could feel my love for her penetrating through the glass.

Normally, I am an extremely laid-back introvert, but this day, as strangers walked by, I told them to look at my new, beautiful daughter. They smiled at and acknowledged my daughter. I tried hard to contain my happiness.

One beautiful gesture that will forever be entrenched in my heart! My mother-in-law rode the bus from North Carolina to Alexandria, Virginia, to see her new granddaughter. She braved her way through snowy and icy weather to bring her granddaughter, receiving blankets and her first new baby clothes. There were twenty-six inches of snow on the ground in Alexandria.

My mother-in-law stayed with us for several days and taught us how to care for a newborn infant. On the bus trip back to North Carolina, due to snow, buses stopped running. She had to spend the night in an isolated bus station in Southern Virginia. Again, her act of kindness and persistence will always be deeply entrenched in my heart. I love you, Mother-in-Law, now and forever!

Still striving for acceptance from my mother, I called to inform her of my good news on two fronts: my new daughter and my graduate degree. It turned out to be another bonehead move on my part. As always, I received negativity from her. She asked, "Are you the baby's real father?" I hung up the telephone.

CHAPTER 45

MY WHITE-COLLAR JOB SEARCH

I refused to focus on my mother's negativity; instead, I focused on finding a good-paying white-collar job to better support my family. At first, I panicked, as it was hard for me trying to quickly transition from a college student and blue-collar worker into securing a good-paying white-collar job. I had to scream out to God to give me strength.

Since I was already employed by the post office, I started applying there for white-collar jobs. My supervisors were notified that I had applied for a white-collar job, and an interested party wanted them to evaluate my job performance. After they received this request, surprisingly, one day, the two white male supervisors called me into the office. They started their conversation by saying, "We suspected something different about you. You think being a mail carrier is beneath you since you have a master's degree? Do you think we are going to give you an excellent job performance rating so you can take our jobs?"

From that day forward, they harassed me daily. A few

uneducated Uncle Toms black male carriers supported the white supervisor in harassing me. For example, one day, to my surprise, I collected a large sum of money on my mail route for a cash-on-delivery (COD) package. COD packages normally had a form for a mail carrier to secure a signature from the customer to show they received the COD package. This form was deliberately not placed in my mail that day.

When I returned to the office, the supervisors were peeping out the office window to see if I submitted the collected COD money to the postal clerk. I registered the full dollar amount with the clerk and asked him for a receipt. As I turned to walk away, I glanced toward the supervisors; their faces had turned as red as stop signs. I waved and smiled. I had just proved to these rednecks and Uncle Toms that I was not a thief. It was ignorant of them to think I would steal such a small amount of money from the federal government. As I left the building to go home, I smiled and thought to myself, *how did these two ignorant, racist rednecks become supervisors?* The answer being white good ole boys.

Another example of harassment, an Uncle Tom black male carrier deliberately put mail for the mail route in reverse order. He thought I would return from the mail route late and give the supervisors a chance to reprimand me. Wrong! I figured out his scheme and delivered the mail to houses and businesses in reverse order and on time. When I returned to the post office, the ignorant black male was standing in the white supervisor's office. He looked stupid in their eyes!

Eventually, I went to post office headquarters to file a complaint for racial discrimination and hostile workplace. I was taken aback when I met another uneducated Uncle Tom black man dressed in a white shirt and tie and carrying a large briefcase. When he opened the briefcase, I noticed he only had his lunch inside. He used poor English during our conversation and boasted mainly how he wore a white shirt and tie to work every day and carried a briefcase. I was not impressed with this illiterate fool.

A few weeks later, he called my house and said he did not find any racial discrimination or a hostile work environment at the post office. Just to make him nervous, I then asked for a written report of his findings. I knew I would never hear from him again, because he was too ignorant to write a report.

In short term, I quickly became disillusioned with my job search. Personnel staff members at most federal government organizations where I applied for a job played games with me. They stated, "You have fulfilled the education requirements. However, you lack professional work experience for the job." I needed them to give me an entry-level professional job so I could gain professional experience. I rode that merry-go-round for months.

MY WHITE-COLLAR JOB TRANSITION

Working for the post office was a step in the right direction in pursuing my dreams and visions. A year later, in late December 1978, I finally got an entry-level position with the then Veterans Administration, now the Department of Veterans Affairs (VA). It was a blessing to have a job where I worked in a climate-controlled building from Monday through Friday. Unlike the post office, with VA, I had all weekends off work.

I was thankful for the job at VA, but it was not a professional, white-collar job with high promotion potential. Every workday during my thirty-minute lunch break, I searched and applied for professional jobs. Over a ten-month period, I applied for over three hundred new jobs. I received daily job rejection letters in the mail at home.

Just when I was about to throw up my hands in defeat, my mind flashed back to when I was sixteen, when I worked on the railroad. Due to extreme heat, I almost fainted swinging a heavy sledgehammer driving iron wedges in wood that supported new railroad tracks. That morning, the white supervisor told me to sit under a shade tree for a few hours to gain my composure. While under that tree, I reflected on the mental and physical strength I inherited from my father and from Grandfather Little. They were two strong males in my life.

After looking back and reflecting on mental and physical strength I learned from my father and from Grandfather Little, I immediately had a change of attitude. They had good reasons to call me a stubborn boy when I was young. I always had the mind-set of never backing down or giving up on my dreams and visions. Drawing from my innate mental and physical strength, I continued to apply for professional jobs.

MY FIRST PROFESSIONAL JOB INTERVIEW

Finally, in late October 1979, I received a telephone call at work to schedule a job interview. That night, I went to Sears and bought a new dark three-piece suit to wear to the interview. The next week, I went on the job interview at VA Headquarters in Washington, DC. The job was in an office that was a direct report to the then administrator of VA, now secretary of VA.

I interviewed with two supervisory levels of management within the Office of Program Evaluation. I was slightly nervous during the interview but could discuss ways to conduct program evaluations. I drew knowledge from my extensive academic background: Peninsula Business College in Newport News, Virginia; undergraduate school at North Carolina Central University in Durham, North Carolina; and the American University Graduate School in Washington, DC.

During the interviews, both managers emphasized they

were looking for a candidate with a master's degree from a highly rated graduate school and who was a Vietnam veteran. The job entailed conducting a program evaluation of the newly established community-based vet center program for Vietnam veterans. I found it was common practice for managers to say, "We will notify you if you are selected for the job."

In the interim, I continued to apply for other federal government jobs. I waited nervously for two months to receive written or verbal communication regarding the program evaluation job. Two weeks before Christmas in 1979, my current supervisor called me to her desk to accept a telephone call. We did not have telephones on our desks on this job. It was the lady supervisor I interviewed with for the program evaluation job. She said, "Ken, congratulations, you have been selected for the job and you will also receive a promotion!"

I screamed out loud in the office at the top of my voice, saying to my new supervisor, "Thank you, thank you, and thank you!"

My current officemates stopped working to observe my insane, out-of-control, happy behavior. When I calmed down, I apologized to them for my outburst in the office. An officemate then said to me, if I am selected for a new professional job, I am going to run around the office then run around some more outside the building. My current supervisor congratulated me in front of the staff and wished me success on my new job.

I was truly grateful and knew God was still working and showing favor in my life. I had faith that God would eventually lift me up to where I belonged. My new professional job title was management analyst. The new job and promotion were indeed blessings and beautiful Christmas presents for me and my family.

REPORTING TO MY
FIRST PROFESSIONAL JOB

On December 27, 1979, I reported to my new job wearing another new suit and tie I bought at Sears. Most staff members were away on Christmas vacation and were scheduled to return to work after New Year's in January 1980.

After New Year's, I was assigned to work on a team with two senior management analysts. Both had incredible analytical and writing skills. They were my immediate mentors. My supervisor paid for several management analysis training classes for me.

MY NEW HANDSOME BABY BOY

Fourteen months after the birth of our daughter, in May 1980, my wife and I were blessed with a handsome baby boy. When the doctor brought him out of the delivery room within minutes after his birth, I felt love welling up inside me. My love for my new son erupted inside me like an active volcano. He was long and lean and had big hands for an infant. I loved holding this bundle of joy in my arms. He constantly smiled at me. I felt the love flowing between us.

After the doctor took my new baby boy away, I made a pledge to myself that my son would have a better life than I did. I committed myself to ensuring he received a college education, developed keen social and interpersonal skills, and traveled domestically and internationally. More importantly, I would impart my wisdom and build mental toughness for him to survive the racist society he would face as a black male.

My mother-in-law rode the bus again from North Carolina to Alexandria, Virginia, to see her new grandson. She commented on his handsome looks. She brought receiving blankets and infant clothes for him. She was the best mother-in-law in the whole wide world.

I thanked God for my new son. I now had two bundles of love, a beautiful daughter and a handsome son. I grudgingly called my mother to inform her of her new grandson. As usual, I did not receive a congratulation from her. I had to keep moving forward. When I returned to work, I passed out cigars and candy to office staff to celebrate my new baby boy. Office managers and staff members congratulated me.

SHOW-AND-TELL TIME ON MY NEW JOB

It was now time to prove myself worthy of my new management analyst job. Although I possessed a master's degree, I immediately realized there was an urgent need to refine my communication skills to excel in this new job. I used my personal funds to pay for night adult education classes. My communication classes included basic English grammar, vocabulary building, writing, and public speaking. The new job taught me that excellent communication skills were key to surviving and excelling in a white-collar job.

The team traveled to numerous states across the country to visit various VA facilities to collect program evaluation data. We conducted personal and telephone interviews with VA staff members to determine if their VA programs followed their program's goals and objectives. The team collected and analyzed data and used it to write program evaluation reports. After the review and approval process, program evaluation reports were approved and provided to program officials, key VA executives, and members of the Congress.

For three years, I worked as a team member and, later, as analyst in charge of a team conducting program evaluations of VA's community-based vet centers for Vietnam Veterans. Personally, it was extremely challenging and yet rewarding for me to support my fellow Vietnam Veterans.

My supervisor recommended me for large cash awards annually and promoted me three years in a row. I worked long hours and weekends to earn these cash awards and promotions, white staff members became extremely jealous and I encountered numerous situations of backstabbing. Suddenly, racism reared its ugly head. The next promotion would have made me a supervisor. My white male officemates received their promotions in a timely fashion. I worked hard, displayed professionalism, and wanted my promotion too.

When my team completed a draft of part two of the Vietnam Veterans program evaluation report, the top office executive wrote to my supervisor and told her that this was the best and most comprehensive evaluation report he had ever read. After the positive remarks about the evaluation report circulated the office, white male managers and officemates started lying and harassing me—it was totally unwarranted. Rumors circulated that I was harassing white employees. Wrong. The top manager called me into his office and interrogated me regarding this unsubstantiated rumor. I asked for facts regarding this claim, and he was speechless.

One day, a white male jokingly told me I was too smart for my own good. I sarcastically thanked him. What he did not know was, it was God's favor shining on me.

A dirty example of people undermining me was when a white male in the office leaked an unofficial copy of part two of the draft evaluation report to his friend who was a staff member for a congressman on Capitol Hill. The top white male executive called me into his office again, lied, and accused me of sending the draft report to the Congress. He could not look me in the eye while telling this lie. This was a setup to make me look bad before office staff and the Congress and degraded my character.

After several more episodes of harassment by white male managers, I eventually filed equal employment opportunity (EEO) complaints against them. After each episode of unfair treatment, I filed more complaints. I initiated this approach after I visited a black clinical psychologist named Dr. Jenkins. He advised me to "stop losing sleep over white managers' racist games."

"Flip the script, keep filing EEOs, and make them lose sleep. Although the EEO process is corrupt, if you keep sending the same names to EEO, eventually, EEO management must focus on your cases. Win or lose, it costs VA and EEO a lot of money to adjudicate discrimination cases."

Eventually, I was labeled as a troublemaker. I ignored this label and proved to them that I was not an Uncle Tom or a docile black man. Although it was hard, I continued to be a hard worker and conducted myself in a very professional manner. To remain at peace at work, I looked to God in heaven and waited for His favor in my life. I dedicated my work for Veterans to God.

In the mid-1980s, there was an extremely limited number of black employees in pay grades GS-14 and above. The glass ceiling was fixed firmly in place in VA. Some of my white counterparts in VA lied and attacked black employees' character to gain favor with racist good ole boys. In my opinion, this was an ongoing practice in VA. If white employees showed they supported white male managers' racist behavior, they were inducted into the racist good ole boys club and promoted. However, there were some white employees who did not embrace racist doctrines; they, too, were passed over for promotions.

CHAPTER 46

BUYING A NEW HOUSE

In August 1983, we moved from the two-bedroom apartment in Alexandria, Virginia, into a large four-bedroom house in Maryland. I used my GI Bill benefits earned from serving in the army to purchase the house. The house was three thousand square feet with a large two-car garage and was built on half an acre of land.

Okay, another bonehead move. I called my mother and shared the good news about our new house. She asked, "Where do you live now?" I responded, "We bought a beautiful house in Maryland." Her next response rocked me back on my heels. She yelled, "Why did you move into the slums of Baltimore?" Before I could respond and tell her I did not live in Baltimore, she hung up the telephone.

That day, I made up my mind to never, never, ever try to impress or gain acceptance from my mother again. Throughout my life, I tried to impress my mother, and each time, she rejected me. And I still carry the pain of her rejection.

PEARL HARBOR DAY FOR MY OFFICE

On December 7, 1987, staff members were called into an all-hands staff meeting. The senior executive dropped a bomb on staff. We were told, effective that day, our office was being dissolved. Staff members stood there in shock and disbelief. The executive assured no one would lose their job; however, staff would be dispersed to different offices within VA central headquarters in Washington, DC.

After thirty-three years of service, I retired from the federal government. To defy odds and demonstrate God's favor on my life, I was eventually promoted as program manager.

CHAPTER 47

SUMMARY OF MY DREAMS AND VISIONS FOR A BETTER LIFE

First, I owe a huge debt of gratitude to God for His blessings and the intestinal fortitude He instilled in me. I now know that all things are possible if you have faith, dream big, and strongly pursue your dreams and visions.

At the beginning of my memoir, I listed a few of my original dreams and visions. I noted, from childhood to adulthood, I nurtured fascinating dreams and visions for a better life. These dreams and visions resonated in my mind and heart both day and night. I accomplished the following dreams and visions to improve my and my family's lives:

- Graduated from high school in 1966 and left home in New London, North Carolina, at the age of seventeen
- Worked in the Newport News Shipyard during the day and attended business school at night for one year
- Served in the military and was stationed in Germany and Vietnam; honorably discharged from the US Army

- Traveled to Hong Kong and Australia for rest and recuperation while stationed in Vietnam

- Graduated from North Carolina Central University in Durham, North Carolina, with a bachelor's degree in political science and public administration; used GI Bill education benefits

- Got married and moved to Arlington, Virginia, to pursue a master's degree

- Graduated from the American University in Washington, DC, with a master's degree in public administration; used GI Bill education benefits

- Secured a high-paying white-collar job with the federal government

- Had two beautiful children, whom I love dearly

- Worked with twenty-one six-year-old Tiger Cub Scouts who later became Boy Scouts, nineteen of whom attained the highest honor in scouting—the prestigious rank of Eagle Scouts

- Organized and traveled to seven foreign countries with Boy Scouts and Explorer Scouts (coed program)

- Completed thirty-four of thirty-seven hours toward a second master's degree in teaching at Bowie State University in Bowie, Maryland

- Traveled to numerous domestic states and cities and international countries and cities as a civilian

I never let go of my dreams and visions from childhood to adulthood. I owe a debt of thanks to people I grew up with in Badin, North Carolina, and New London, North Carolina. They helped me forge my personality and determination. I am a product of these environments.

Again, I hope and pray that my memoir encourages people of all backgrounds and ages who are subjected to physical, verbal, and domestic abuse and racism to stay the course in pursuing their dreams and visions. Breaking these horrible cycles starts with you. Please do not let fear become your enemy. I will always remember what a loving person once said to me: "If you cannot see past your circumstances, then your circumstances become your destiny."

Please reach out to God, and He will reach back to embrace you during your life's journey.

ABOUT THE AUTHOR

OF "TALKING TO GREEN TREE LEAVES"

Kenneth "Ken" L. Little Sr. was born and raised in rural North Carolina. His family experienced financial hardship during the 1950s and 1960s. Segregation and societal racism were norms. The worst hardship occurred when Ken's father, a hardworking man, was laid off from his decent-paying blue-collar job. From ages eight through seventeen, Ken contributed money by working menial jobs, such as working in cotton fields, caddying on a golf course, being a greens-keeper, and working railroad construction.

Ken's mother was a stay-at-home wife. She was narcissistic and suffered from an untreated mental health condition. She often said giving birth to Ken caused her nervous breakdown. She constantly verbally and physically abused him. Further, Ken believes the man who raised him was not his biological father. This belief was fostered by small-town people's gossip. Ken's parents often told him that he would never amount to anything in life, and because of this, Ken became very shy and had low self-esteem. However, his parents' behavior and racism did not stop him from nurturing his dreams, visions, and desire for a better life.

Growing up, Ken spent countless hours sitting in a tall

sycamore tree, talking to its green tree leaves about a better life. In retrospect, Ken believes it was God speaking, encouraging and comforting him in the tall tree. Being persistent and resilient, Ken graduated from high school, served in the army in Germany and Vietnam, earned his bachelor's and master's degrees, and retired from a white-collar job with the federal government.

Resilience, persistence, and prayer are keys to breaking abuse cycles in families and racism in society. Everyone, especially children, deserve to live in a peaceful household and a chance for a better life. With God's help, Ken survived and thrived.

You can too!